Praise fc

Tuesdays at t

An IndieBound Next pick

"There is a warmth here that is utterly irresistible, both in
Celie as the plucky, resourceful protagonist . . . and the
maternal, protective nature of her guardian castle. . . .
Readers will be . . . under the castle's spell." —*BCCB*

"Adventure stories fans will enjoy this as much as children
who wear their wizard cloaks proudly." —*SLJ*

"These kids are clever, as is George's lively adventure.
May pique castle envy." —*Kirkus Reviews*

"This story puts an unexpected spin on the typical princess tale.
Readers will root equally for crafty Celie and for her castle, a truly
unique and memorable 'pet.'" —*Library Media Connection*

"Jessica Day George's princess stories never fail to enchant,
and her latest novel . . . is great fun." —*The Salt Lake Tribune*

"A spunky main character, plenty of intrigue and witty
dialogue. Pair that with the castle featured as a character in
the story, and it's a winning combination." —*Deseret News*

"Jessica Day George . . . has created a charming,
adventurous story with a spirit that will appeal to fans of Kate
DiCamillo's *The Tale of Despereaux*." —Shelf Awareness

BOOKS BY JESSICA DAY GEORGE

Dragon Slippers
Dragon Flight
Dragon Spear

Sun and Moon, Ice and Snow

Princess of the Midnight Ball
Princess of Glass
Princess of the Silver Woods

Tuesdays at the Castle

Tuesdays
at the
Castle

JESSICA DAY GEORGE

BLOOMSBURY

NEW YORK LONDON NEW DELHI SYDNEY

First published in the United States of America in October 2011
by Bloomsbury Books for Young Readers
Paperback edition published in October 2012
www.bloomsburykids.com

For information about permission to reproduce selections from this book, write to
Permissions, Bloomsbury BFYR, 175 Fifth Avenue, New York, New York 10010

The Library of Congress has cataloged the hardcover edition as follows:
George, Jessica Day.
Tuesdays at the castle / by Jessica Day George.—1st U.S. ed.
p.   cm.
Summary: Eleven-year-old Princess Celie lives with her parents, the king and queen,
and her brothers and sister at Castle Glower, which adds rooms or stairways or secret
passageways most every Tuesday, and when the king and queen are ambushed while
travelling, it is up to Celie—the castle's favorite—with her secret knowledge of its
never-ending twists and turns, to protect their home and save their kingdom.
ISBN 978-1-59990-644-7 (hardcover)
[1. Fairy tales. 2. Castles—Fiction. 3. Princesses—Fiction.
4. Kings, queens, rulers, etc.—Fiction.] I. Title.
PZ8.G3295Tu2011   [Fic]—dc23   2011016739

ISBN 978-1-59990-917-2 (paperback)

Book design by Donna Mark
Typeset by Westchester Book Composition
Printed in the U.S.A. by Quad/Graphics, Fairfield, Pennsylvania
2 4 6 8 10 9 7 5 3 1

For Melanie:
Editor extraordinaire!

Tuesdays
at the
Castle

Chapter
1

⟡

Whenever Castle Glower became bored, it would grow a new room or two. It usually happened on Tuesdays, when King Glower was hearing petitions, so it was the duty of the guards at the front gates to tell petitioners the only two rules the Castle seemed to follow.

Rule One: The throne room was always to the east. No matter where you were in the Castle, if you kept heading east you would find the throne room eventually. The only trick to this was figuring out which way east was, especially if you found yourself in a windowless corridor. Or the dungeon.

This was the reason that most guests stuck with Rule Two: If you turned left three times and climbed through the next window, you'd end up in the kitchens, and one of the staff could lead you to the throne room or wherever you needed to go.

Celie only used Rule Two when she wanted to steal a

treat from the kitchens, and Rule One when she wanted to watch her father at work. Her father was King Glower the Seventy-ninth, and like him, Celie always knew which way was east.

And also like him, Celie truly loved Castle Glower. She never minded being late for lessons because the corridor outside her room had become twice as long, and she certainly didn't mind the new room in the south wing that had a bouncy floor. Even if you could only get to it by climbing through the fireplace of the winter dining hall.

King Glower the Seventy-ninth, on the other hand, valued punctuality and didn't enjoy being late for dinner because the Castle had built a new corridor that ran from the main hall under the courtyard to the pastures, and all the sheep had wandered inside to chew the tapestries. He also didn't particularly like waiting for hours for the Ambassador of Bendeswe, only to find that the Castle had removed the door to the ambassador's room, trapping the man inside. Of course, the king had to admit that there was usually some strange logic to the Castle's movements. The Ambassador of Bendeswe, for instance, had turned out to be a spy, and the sheep . . . well, that had all been mere whim; but there was still logic to be found if you looked hard enough. King Glower admitted this freely, and he made it clear that he respected the Castle. He had to; otherwise he would no longer be king.

The Castle didn't seem to care if you were descended from a royal line, or if you were brave or intelligent. No,

Castle Glower picked kings based on some other criteria all its own. Celie's father, Glower the Seventy-ninth, was the tenth in their family to bear that name, a matter of tremendous pride throughout the land. His great-great-great-great-great-great-great-great-grandfather had become king when Glower the Sixty-ninth's only heir had turned out to be a nincompoop. Legend had it that the Castle had repeatedly steered the old king's barber to the throne room via a changing series of corridors for days until the Royal Council had him declared the next king, while the young man who should have been Glower the Seventieth found himself head-down in a haystack after having been forcibly ejected from the Castle through the water closet.

King Glower the Seventy-ninth, Lord of the Castle, Master of the Brine Sea, and Sovereign of the Land of Sleyne, knew when to leave well enough alone. He married the beautiful daughter of the Royal Wizard when the Castle guided them into the same room and then sealed the doors for a day. He paid attention when the Castle gave people larger rooms or softer chairs. When his older son, Bran, kept finding his room full of books and astrolabes, while his second son Rolf's bedroom was moved next to the throne room, King Glower sent Bran to the College of Wizardry, and declared Rolf his heir.

And when little Celie was sick, and the Castle filled her room with flowers, King Glower agreed with it. Everybody loved Celie, the fourth and most delightful of the royal children.

Chapter 2

⟨⟨~⟩⟩

"Everyone hates me," Celie grumbled.

"No one hates you," her sister, Lilah, said soothingly. "But you do have a tendency to bounce."

"There's nothing wrong with bouncing," Celie insisted.

"Very true," her brother Rolf said, coming into the room. "Let's bounce right now!"

Grinning at Lilah in a way that was sure to irritate her, he took hold of Celie's hands and they began to jump up and down in place. Celie forgot to pout, and laughed as they jumped. Rolf could always make her laugh.

Lilah tossed her dark hair to show Rolf that he was being silly, and went to the window to look out. They were in Lilah's room, which was quite large and grand, and straddled a narrow bit of the north wing. There were windows on one side that looked out on the main courtyard, and on the other side was a balcony that hung over a sort of atrium with a fountain in the center of it. Lilah was at the courtyard windows, checking on their parents' travel carriage, which was being stocked with lap rugs and novels, prior to the king and queen taking a journey.

Celie stopped jumping.

"Done, then?" Rolf collapsed on Lilah's bed, knocking several of the many small cushions onto the floor. "You do like to bounce, don't you, Cel?"

"Not anymore," Celie muttered.

"I'm going to have to start climbing through that fireplace into the new room," Rolf went on, not having heard her. "Get in some practice." He held his chest and panted.

Celie watched a trunk the size of a coffin being carried out by two burly footmen and loaded into the luggage cart that waited beside the carriage. It would indeed be a long journey her parents were taking, and they weren't taking her with them. Which is why she had been in the throne room, getting underfoot, until Lilah had lured her upstairs with the promise of caramel apples. "And there's no caramel apples," she griped.

"Caramel apples!" Rolf leaped back off the bed. "Where?"

"There will be," Lilah said with great patience. "Once Mother and Father are gone. Cook said we could make them ourselves tonight after supper."

"Excellent," Rolf said. "I do like a caramel apple. Also, with chocolate on. And cinnamon sugar." He rubbed his hands together eagerly. He was tall and blond, with endearingly crooked front teeth.

Celie, who was also blond but small (she was only just eleven), gave her brother a dark look. "I'd rather go with Daddy and Mummy," she said, knowing she sounded like a brat. "But if you just want to fill your stomach, you can stay here."

"Cecelia!" Lilah's voice was sharp. She was tall, and when she stood shoulder to shoulder with Rolf their resemblance to the king and queen was both striking and intimidating. "You know very well that we cannot go to the College of Wizardry, so there is no need to be rude about it."

"I know that *Rolf* can't go," Celie grumped. Her tutor had explained that a king and his heir never traveled together, in case of an accident. "But I don't understand why *I* can't go and see Bran graduate."

"Because Father said no, and Father is the king," Lilah said.

"Well, it's a silly reason," Celie said, knowing that she sounded even more childish but not caring.

She ducked between them and out of the room. She paused for just a moment in the hallway, but she heard Lilah say, "Oh, let her go, Rolf. She's determined to be difficult."

So Celie stomped off down the hall. She found some stairs, and climbed them, and then a hallway and more stairs and just kept going. She didn't have her atlas with her, and wasn't sure she'd ever seen this particular staircase, but she was trying too hard to hang on to her disagreeable mood and told herself she didn't care if she got lost.

Not that she thought she'd get lost. All of the royal children knew the rules very well, and besides, it was fairly obvious that the Castle liked them. But Celie was trying to make an atlas of Castle Glower, the first ever, and normally carried colored pencils and paper with her to sketch anything she hadn't seen before. So far she had three hundred pages of maps, and could get to most of the major rooms (winter and summer dining halls, chapel, library, throne room) in record time as long as the Castle wasn't bored and looking to stretch.

But all she found at the top of the stairs was a small round room. Still, she didn't want to stomp back down the stairs just yet, so she stayed to explore. The room had windows that looked in all four directions, and she could see the mountains around Castle Glower's small, bowl-shaped valley. There was a gold spyglass mounted in each of the windows. She peered through the eastern one and saw the slopes of the Indigo Mountains, dotted with small villages that were populated mainly by goatherds.

She looked to the south, where the main road wound between the mountains toward Sleyne City, where the College of Wizardry was. It made her sad all over again, so she turned to the center of the room.

The only thing in the room, other than the spyglasses, was a large table with some things scattered across it. She found a coil of rope, a book, a compass, and a large tin that proved to be full of hard ginger biscuits. Celie took one of the latter. It was the kind of sweet that often got passed around at Midwinter, when guests would show up unexpectedly and Cook didn't have time to make fresh biscuits.

"How long have these been here?" Celie frowned at the biscuit. She had nearly broken a tooth biting into it. It could have been there for a hundred years, and would probably be edible for a hundred more.

She went to the window and tossed it down to a flat section of roof a little ways away. It broke into pieces, which some sparrows pounced on and then wittered off a moment later in disgust. She looked down into the main courtyard, and saw her parents standing before the travel carriage. Rolf and Lilah were there, and the steward and others of the Castle staff.

"Oh, no!" Her parents were leaving, and she wasn't there to tell them good-bye! She had thought about hiding until they left, to make them regret leaving, but now she wanted very badly to hug both her parents. She raced out of the round room and looked down the twisting staircase in despair.

She leaned against the wall, suddenly tired from all the emotions of the day, and realized that she was leaning against another door. Had it always been there? It was narrow, and she pushed it open listlessly, certain that it would just prove to be a small cupboard, and then she would have to hurry even faster to catch her parents.

But to her delight it was a slide. A stone slide that curved down, following the path of the staircase. Celie sat at the top, tucked her skirts around her knees, and pushed off.

The slide curved and spun and Celie laughed as it whizzed her down through the Castle and deposited her right at the edge of the courtyard, no more than a dozen paces from where her parents were standing.

Celie scrambled to her feet and tidied her gown and hair, not sure if her parents would be angry with her or not. She had been hanging around the throne room, and their private chambers, all morning, hoping that if she got in the way often enough, they would relent and take her along. Finally, her father had yelled to Lilah that she needed to "do something with that little sister of hers."

"Come here, darling," said Queen Celina now, holding out her arms.

Celie ran to her mother and hugged her tight. The queen always smelled like strawberries, and everyone said that she was as beautiful at forty as she had been when the king had married her. Tall and slender and stately, with her long dark hair pinned up with gold combs, she wore a travel dress of soft green that set off her eyes.

"I'll miss you," Celie mumbled into her mother's waist.

"I'll miss you, too," said the queen. "I'll miss all my darlings. But we won't be gone long. We're just going to see Bran graduate, and then we'll all be home again."

"Bran, too?"

"Bran, too," Queen Celina assured her. "He will be the new Royal Wizard when we return." She smiled sadly. The old Royal Wizard, her father, had died two years before.

Then the queen turned Celie around and pushed her

gently toward the king. King Glower was trying to look stern, but his face soon melted and he held out his arms to his little girl. "Come on, then, Celia-delia," he said.

Celie jumped into his arms and buried her face in her father's neck. His travel robe had a fur collar, and it tickled her nose. "I still want to go," she said.

"Not this time, sweetheart," her father said. "When you are older, I will take you to Sleyne City to see all the sights."

"I could see the sights now," Celie said reasonably. "With you and Mummy and Bran."

"Another time," her father said. He set her down on the cobbles and disentangled her arms from his neck. "Besides, the Castle needs you. I wouldn't want to make it angry by taking you away for too long."

"Oh, pooh!" But Celie couldn't help being a bit flattered. She liked to imagine that the Castle really did like her, and it was nice that her father had noticed.

"Besides, somebody's got to keep me in line," Rolf said easily, putting an arm around her shoulders and drawing her to his side.

"Don't worry, Mother," Lilah said, kissing the queen's cheek. "I'll look after both of them."

Celie and Rolf shared an eye roll. They knew what that meant: Lilah would act queenly and matronly by turns, and order them to eat in the summer dining hall in full court dress every night. But she'd also admonish them constantly to eat their vegetables and not slurp their soup. Celie wondered how long it would take her parents to reach Sleyne

City, see Bran graduate, and bring him home. More than two weeks of Lilah's mothering and they should all run mad.

But now her parents were in the carriage, and waving, and the carriage was moving out of the Castle gates and down the long road to Sleyne City. They waved until the luggage cart and the ranks of soldiers on horseback blocked the royal traveling coach from view.

"All right, both of you," Lilah said briskly. "Back into the Castle. It's a bit chilly out, and I don't want you to catch cold."

"Lilah," said Rolf.

"Yes, dear?"

"Tag! You're it!" Rolf whacked her on the arm and took off at a run.

Lilah shrieked in outrage, but Celie didn't wait around to see what happened next. A well-played game of tag could go on for days in Castle Glower, and Lilah had been known to cheat.

Chapter
3

It was a Tuesday, and Celie was waiting to see what the Castle would do.

Her parents had been gone nearly two weeks, and things had settled into a routine, with Rolf taking on whatever minor royal duties he could, Lilah in charge of the servants, and Celie working on her atlas. Their parents had left on a Thursday, and other than Celie's discovery of the little turret with the spyglasses at each window, the Castle hadn't done much.

The next Tuesday had been fourteen-year-old Rolf's first day hearing petitions, and there had not been any problems of a Castle-based nature. On the other hand, all the villagers, farmers, and shepherds from miles around had come to present land disputes and water disputes and family grievances, hoping that Rolf would rule in their favor out of naiveté. Some people brought out issues that King Glower had already ruled on, slyly looking for a different outcome, and even tried to invent disasters (floods, goat pox epidemics) so that the Crown would give them money in recompense.

Despite his son's youth, however, there was a very good reason why King Glower had paid attention when the Castle had showed a preference for Rolf over Bran. Rolf was not stupid. He had been sitting in the throne room by his father's side since he was a small child, and he knew most of the people who lived in the valley.

For instance, Rolf remembered that Osric Swann had been paid handsomely to rebuild his mill after the last flood, and knew that there hadn't been another flood since. He knew that Pogue Parry got into a fight with someone nearly every week, that it was almost always Pogue's fault, and that there was no earthly reason for the Crown to be involved. He knew that Delcoe Ross's goats were often thin and sickly, but that was because Delcoe Ross was a skinflint and barely fed them enough to keep them alive.

"Master Ross, kindly go home and feed your livestock some oats," Rolf said to the sour-faced man. "The Crown has already paid you on a number of occasions for their medical expenses. If you haven't used that money on yourself, I recommend you use it on them." He casually reached one hand under the throne and poked Celie.

She slapped his hand away. She was crouching under the boxlike seat of the throne while she sketched the hallway that led from the servants' quarters to the throne room. The door to it was hidden by a tapestry behind the throne on this end, and inside a broom closet at the servants' end. It took a number of twists and turns, and occasionally sprouted doors to other rooms. She had promised the housekeeper that she would map it out and make copies for some of the newer maids. It was the fastest way to the throne room, but you had to follow it straight or you'd end up in the library or Lilah's room. Which was fine, except on Mondays, when the throne room needed to be cleaned. The housekeeper didn't like the idea of new maids getting lost and wandering off who-knows-where.

"Now what?" Rolf barely bothered to keep the irritation out of his voice. Several of the petitioners from last week were back with the same problems, and Rolf had whispered to Celie earlier that they must think him terribly stupid to petition him all over again.

"Just wondering, Your Highness, if Princess Delilah is at home," said Pogue Parry.

Celie would recognize his voice anywhere. Pogue was easily the handsomest young man in Glower Valley, which was presumably why he ended up in so many fights. All he had to do was look at a girl, and she would completely forget her beau and run after Pogue. Even Celie wasn't immune to his smiles, and poked her head out from under the throne to grin at him.

Pogue winked at her. "Hullo there, Princess Cecelia. Want to help me find your lovely, lovely sister?"

"No, she does not," Rolf said crossly. "And Lilah's busy. Next!"

"I might have another issue to discuss," Pogue said lazily.

"If it concerns either of my sisters, the answer is no," Rolf said.

Pogue smiled his mischievous grin, and Celie found herself sighing a little. She clambered out from under the throne, her bundle of papers in hand. She was done making a master map of the passageway; now all that remained was to copy it a few times.

"I'll take you to Del—Lilah," she said.

Nobody but Pogue or very elderly courtiers called Celie's sister by her full name. It was as if Pogue savored the name. Celie made a mental note to ask her parents why. They would be home that night, or the next day at the latest.

"Your parents should be home soon," Pogue said, startling her as his words echoed her thoughts.

"Yes, we expect them at any minute, really," Celie replied, leading him down a long passageway. If they turned right and took the next flight of stairs, they should end up near the small dining hall, where Lilah would be overseeing the table setting for dinner. The Councilors of Finance and Public Works would be joining them that night.

"I like your parents," Pogue said unexpectedly.

She goggled at him. "You have to," she pointed out. "They're the king and queen."

"I *don't* have to, actually," Pogue said with a quick grin.

"I just have to respect them . . . not even that! All one really has to do is obey royalty. But I like them all the same. If you ever need anything, you know where m'father's shop is, don't you?"

"Of course. He's the only blacksmith in the village," Celie said. Something about this conversation felt strange. Not that Pogue wasn't sincere: just the opposite. And that was part of it. Pogue was never sincere, or at least, he was never serious. He usually just teased.

"Good girl," he said, and tweaked one of her curls. They had reached the small dining room, and could see Lilah through the doors, ordering around a footman with a chair. "O fair Delilah!" Pogue went down on one knee, and Celie left him to flirt and Lilah to flutter.

She took the map to her room and carefully copied it five times. Then she went to the housekeeper's sitting room and delivered the copies to Ma'am Housekeeper, as everyone called her. Celie had kept the master copy to add to her own atlas, and on her way to her room she began to muse about how many pages it might be when it was finally completed. But how could she ever finish? The Castle grew new rooms every week, and occasionally got rid of others that were no longer used. Already there was a series of closets in her maps that were now gone, since the linens Ma'am Housekeeper had kept in them had been eaten by moths.

"Someone should help me," Celie muttered. "But no one else seems to care. They just shrug and say that the Castle does what it does and . . . huh."

Maybe the Castle really was doing what it wanted, she finally realized. And to her. She'd been aiming for her room, but instead found herself at the foot of the stairs that led to the tower with the four spyglasses. It was as if the Castle had turned the corridors around to lead her there.

"Fine, then," she agreed, and went up to the little room.

Nothing had changed. Celie set her notebook and pencil case on the table and looked around. There was the rope, the biscuits, the book, and the spyglasses mounted on the windowsills. She took a moment to sketch the room, and made notes about where she had found it both times. Then she went to one of the spyglasses and peered through. She could see the main road, and hovering over it a plume of dust that signaled the approach of someone traveling toward the Castle at top speed.

She squinched her face and tried to look harder. Was that her parents' carriage? And if it was their carriage, where was the luggage cart? The attendant soldiers on their horses?

Celie found a ring on the spyglass that adjusted the view, and toyed with it until the vehicle in the dust cloud came into better focus. It *was* the royal carriage, but it was unaccompanied by luggage or soldiers, and moving far too fast for comfort. This was not right.

Celie raced back the way she had come and burst into the throne room, where she skidded to a halt amid the curious gazes of the petitioners and the amused look of her brother. He clearly wanted a break, and looked expectantly at her as she straightened her skirts and hair.

"In a rush, Cel?"

"I need to talk to you," she said, hurrying over to the throne. "In private. Right now."

"Thank heavens," Rolf muttered. "A five-minute break, everyone," he announced loudly.

They ducked through a door behind a tapestry of a sea serpent and into the small study their father often used to meet with his Council. Refreshments had been set on the table there, and Rolf started to pour a glass of water before he saw her expression and froze.

"What is it?"

"I found a room with a spyglass and was looking at the road. I can see the carriage coming, but it's moving awfully fast and there aren't any soldiers with it. Or luggage." She said it all in a rush.

"What? Are you sure it's *the* carriage? Mother and Father's carriage?"

"Yes," Celie said.

Only now she wasn't so sure. True, it was a large carriage, but there were probably dozens like it in the kingdom. She hadn't actually seen the royal crest on the doors; it was too dusty for that. What if she made a fuss and she was wrong?

"You'd better show me," Rolf said.

Celie always appreciated the fact that her brother treated her like an equal. She just hoped that she wasn't abusing his trust now, as she guided him to the foot of the winding stair that led to the Spyglass Tower, as Celie had dubbed it in her head.

"Up here."

Rolf took the stairs two at a time despite his robes of state, and was soon peering through the south-mounted spyglass at the road.

"You're right, that's their carriage," Rolf said. "It just passed through the village, which means it should be here in a minute. We'd better go down to meet it."

It was a matter of minutes before they were in the courtyard. Rolf sent a servant to find Lilah while he and Celie paced up and down the cobblestones.

They didn't have to wait very long. Lilah arrived at the same time as the carriage, which came barreling through the main gate and lurched to a halt just a few paces away. The horses were lathered and blowing, and the carriage was filthy and battered.

"Is that an arrow?"

It was Pogue who asked. He'd come with Lilah, of course, and was the only one of them who could speak. Because there *was* an arrow stuck in the carriage door. In fact, several arrows studded the carriage, and now that the horses had stopped, Celie noticed that one of them was a gray while the rest were the chestnuts preferred by the king, so they'd had to replace one of the horses somewhere along the way.

"Mummy?" Celie took a hesitant step toward the carriage, but Lilah pulled her back.

The door crashed open and a man half fell out. It was one of the royal guard—no, it was their sergeant. He was streaked with dirt and blood, and his left arm hung in a sling made out of a silk scarf. One of the queen's silk scarves.

"Your Highness," he said when he saw Rolf, and straightened with an effort. "I mean, Your Majesty." He bent his head stiffly. "I regret to inform you that King Glower, your father, is dead."

"And Mummy?" Celie's voice was so small she wondered if he had heard her.

He had.

"I regret to say that Her Majesty is dead as well."

Chapter
4

⁂

Bandits, in the pass," Sergeant Avery explained.

They had all stumbled into the throne room, dismissed the petitioners, and summoned the Council instead. Avery slumped in a chair, but Rolf refused to sit on the throne. He'd sat in it all day, with ease, but now Celie noticed that he couldn't even look at it. Avery kept trying to rise, but he was exhausted and injured, and they all pushed him back down whenever he started up.

"They were waiting for us. As soon as we reached the narrowest stretch they attacked from both sides. Arrows thick as a swarm of bees, most of my men down before they had time to draw sword. The carriage horses spooked, but one of them tripped and broke a leg, otherwise I'd have had to walk here."

"How did you escape?" Lilah's voice was thin, but calm.

"Hit my head on a rock when my horse went down.

That's how I wrenched my shoulder as well." He took a long drink from the cup a maid offered him. "When I woke, it was all over. Men dead everywhere, horses scattered, a disaster." He drank again, avoiding looking at the throne. Or Rolf.

"And did you actually see Their Majesties' bodies?" This from one of the Councilors.

"No . . . ," Avery said slowly. "I thought I saw the queen's green gown, over beneath some of the mess from the luggage cart. Prince Bran had been riding, and I saw his horse, dead, on the road."

"But the king?" The Councilor—Lord Sefton, who was barely older than Bran—leaned in, eager, and Celie felt a flutter of hope rise in her heart as well.

"No," Sergeant Avery said in a grim voice. His eyes flicked to Celie, and she looked steadily back. "I'm afraid . . . I didn't see him. . . . But I found this in the dust."

Celie's heart plummeted.

Lord Sefton sat back, the shock and strain making him look much older. Sergeant Avery was holding up the Griffin Ring; the winged lion was fashioned from gold with emerald-chip eyes that seemed to wink in the light of the room. Celie's father, like every other King Glower, was given the Griffin Ring at his coronation. It was to be worn always as a reminder of the king's duties, and Celie had never seen her father without it. She wasn't even entirely certain that it *could* be taken off. Rolf had once told her that it was enchanted, and could only be removed after the king's death.

She had thought he was teasing then.

Sergeant Avery was holding the ring out to Rolf, but he wouldn't take it. Finally, the elderly Lord Feen held out a shaking hand, and the sergeant dropped the heavy ring into it. A shiver passed through Celie.

"Nevertheless, we'll send a search party," the Emissary to Foreign Lands said in a brisk voice. "To see if there are any more survivors, or anything left to salvage."

"Of course, my lord," Sergeant Avery said, straightening. "I'll lead the party myself." He looked at Rolf now, and started to get up, but Rolf waved him down again.

"Thank you, Sergeant," Rolf said. "But first we'll have a physician look at your wounds." He sent one of the footmen for the castle physician, and one of the guards to gather a search party, armed.

"That is a noble idea, Lord Emissary," Lord Feen said in his quavering voice. "If it is true they are dead, then it will be good if they can bring back the bodies of our lamented King Glower the Seventy-ninth and his queen."

Lilah made a little mewing noise at the word "bodies," and Celie clutched at her sister's waist. She felt like she was in a nightmare, and hoped desperately to wake up. Pogue Parry, who was hovering behind them, stepped forward and put one hand on Lilah's shoulder, and one on Celie's. His hands were large and very warm, and Celie was glad that Pogue had come to flirt with Lilah that day.

"And of course," Lord Feen went on, "if it is true that the king and queen are dead, there are arrangements that must be made. Castle Glower cannot go very long without a king. Plans for your coronation—"

"No," Rolf said. "We must be certain that my parents are . . . not alive, first."

Lilah made another mewing noise.

Celie felt tears slipping down her face and wetting the front of her gown. How could Rolf stand there and suggest that their parents might be dead? How *could* he?

A sob burst out before she could stop it, and Pogue's hand tightened on her shoulder. Lilah had both her arms around Celie, and now she bent and rested her cheek on Celie's hair. Tears dripped from Lilah's eyes onto Celie's cheek, and she didn't brush them away.

"I will do my best to find them, Your Maj—Your Highness," Sergeant Avery said. He stood up, and this time no one stopped him.

"Thank you, Sergeant," Rolf said. "I am glad that I can rely on you."

The physician had come, and now Sergeant Avery followed the man out, so that he could be examined in private. The rest of the Councilors clustered together, whispering and eyeing Celie and her brother and sister. Rolf stepped in front of the throne and cleared his throat. They all fell silent.

"Whoever did this must be brought to justice," Rolf said, his voice grim. "I will be sending a full complement of soldiers with Sergeant Avery, as soon as possible, to look for my father and mother, but also to hunt down—"

"Your Highness, please," interrupted the Emissary. "Let us not mar this sad occasion with talk of revenge. This can only lead to more tragedy."

Rolf stared at him incredulously. "You don't think that the attack on *your king* merits retaliation?"

The Emissary shook his head, sighing softly as though Rolf had disappointed him. "Until such time as we can verify the fate of the king and queen, and until those who perished in this attack are properly mourned and laid to rest, there is nothing more to be done," he announced. "For now, you are all dismissed."

Rolf looked at him for a moment in shock, then he stepped down off the dais and nodded curtly to Pogue, who bowed and moved back. Rolf put his arms around Lilah and Celie, and everyone else left the room, leaving the three siblings to their grief.

Chapter
5

The country of Sleyne mourned, and Castle Glower mourned with them. It didn't grow new rooms, didn't stretch corridors, and when the bright banners that hung from the Castle walls were taken down, it didn't replace them. Courtiers and commoners alike filed through the Castle with black armbands to bow and curtsy and murmur condolences to Celie and Rolf and Lilah, who refused to accept them. Not yet.

Celie didn't have a dark-colored gown, which fretted her, and she worried that people would think she wasn't showing proper respect. Her parents and brother were missing, and people had died, and she was wearing pale gray. It seemed silly to be concerned over such a thing, but at the same time, she had little else to do.

The morning after the terrible news had come, Lilah had helped Celie into the gray gown, made for a war remembrance ceremony a few months before, and wound a piece of black silk around her waist for a sash. The seamstresses were working quickly to make her a more suitable black gown, however, and one for Lilah as well, although Lilah already looked elegant in a black satin gown she had worn to their great-aunt's funeral the year before. Celie was growing so fast that her funeral gown couldn't be fastened up at all, and as it was, the gray gown was an inch too short and chafed under her arms.

But when Celie went to the throne room two days after the news had come, she found other things to worry about than her clothes. Rolf was sitting on a low stool that had been placed to the side of the throne. He was wearing a black tunic of their father's that was the right length and width in the shoulders, but far too loose about the middle. His face was pale, and there were dark circles under his eyes.

All the Councilors were clustered around, whispering to one another and eyeing Rolf, and there were two couriers from neighboring countries standing before the dais, looking patient. Celie could tell that this was more worrisome than her ill-fitting gown and Rolf's too-large borrowed tunic. She knew if anyone saw her, she would probably be sent out, so she sidled along the wall to where Lilah was standing with Pogue Parry.

In the days since their parents had been attacked, Pogue had become the royal family's staunchest ally. He had turned up at the gates of Castle Glower for the past two mornings, properly and soberly dressed in a dark gray tunic with a black armband. He had been quiet and respectful to Rolf and Lilah, and kind and friendly to Celie. He stopped flirting with Lilah (and the maids, and the girls from the village) and ran errands for Lilah instead, helped her arrange mourning bands for the servants, organized the townsfolk gathering to hold vigil, and was quickly becoming indispensible.

"What's happening?" Celie took Lilah's hand and gave it a squeeze.

"You wouldn't understand," Lilah whispered. "Go to the kitchens and get some lunch."

Celie let go of her sister's hand and slipped behind her to stand by Pogue instead. "What's happening?"

"The ambassador to Vhervhine is here," Pogue whispered, pointing with his chin at a large man in plum-colored velvet and heavy boots standing before the throne. "He brought some interesting news."

Celie's pulse raced. "What? Do they have news of my parents?"

Pogue took her hand gently. "No. I'm sorry," he murmured, leaning down so he could speak softly to her. "Vhervhine wishes to send an Emissary to the . . . funeral . . . next week."

"But that's good." She straightened a little, trying to look more like a princess. "Isn't it? Shouldn't they send an Emissary? Even if there isn't really a funeral." Celie held fast to this hope, that Sergeant Avery would return, escorting her parents, and the funeral preparations would be used instead for a grand celebration.

"They are planning to send one of the royal princes," Pogue said. "Prince Khelsh. Which means that he will have dozens of armed guards, plus servants and advisers and also a minister of state."

"Isn't Prince Khelsh the mean one?" Celie wrinkled her nose, trying to remember. The Vhervhish people were rather warlike as it was, but the second son, she thought it was Khelsh, was supposedly a real horror.

"That's the one," Pogue said under his breath.

The Vhervhish ambassador was glaring at them. His tunic buttoned up the left side of his breast, all the way to his throat in the singular style of his people, which Celie always thought looked very uncomfortable. Judging by the sour expression on the man's face, he was either uncomfortable or quite simply didn't want to be there at all.

"Ew," Celie muttered. Pogue squeezed her hand a little in reply.

"And my prince, also, he will be coming with many fine gifts and many fine servants," another man said. He flourished his hands a great deal as he talked, which made the trailing sleeves of his silk tunic flap, and he looked at the throne and the walls rather than Rolf. "He is a very, very man, our beloved Prince Lulath." He said this to one of the carved pillars that supported the throne room's vaulted ceiling.

"Lulath?" Celie tried to remember where she'd heard that name before. Or place the speaker's accent.

"This is the ambassador from Grath," Pogue murmured. "Lulath is the third son, I think he said."

Celie let out a small snort of laughter. Lulath of Grath? Rolf gave her a stern look, and now the Grathian ambassador glared.

Then Rolf's gaze cleared, and he beckoned to Celie. "Sister, would you come forward?"

"Yes . . . brother," she said. She felt her cheeks burn, and walked rather slowly to Rolf's side.

"My younger sister, Princess Cecelia," Rolf said, presenting her to the two ambassadors. "Cecelia dear, here is the ambassador from our dear neighbors in Vhervhine, and here is the ambassador from our equally dear neighbors in Grath."

Celie nodded politely to both men, who bowed. The Vhervhish ambassador was rather perfunctory about it, but the man from Grath did so with many flourishes and sidelong looks, as though checking to see who was watching.

"Princess Cecelia is quite the best of us when it comes to knowing the Castle," Rolf said to the ambassadors. Then he turned to Celie. "I want to make sure that our two princely visitors and their attendants are properly cared for during their stay, Cecelia. Would you be so kind as to ask the Castle to provide them with suites of rooms, as befitting their status and as suited to their needs?"

Celie just goggled at Rolf for a minute or two. She could

no more ask the Castle to provide rooms for the princes than stand on her head on the roof of the Spyglass Tower! No matter how well it liked you or how nicely you asked, the Castle was far more inclined to do the opposite, if it did anything at all.

She was about to point this out to Rolf when she noticed the two ambassadors. They were both leaning forward, eager to hear what she had to say. The Vhervhish ambassador had a faint sneer on his face, though, and the Grathian's eyes were narrowed with speculation.

"Of course, dear brother," Celie said sweetly. "It would be my pleasure."

"Thank you, Cecelia darling," Rolf replied. His expression was suddenly sly. "They will each have twenty-five men with them—that *includes* men-at-arms, advisers, and servants."

This last, she realized, was strictly for the benefit of the ambassadors. Off to the side, Celie saw Pogue raise his eyebrows, and heard the Vhervhish ambassador draw a breath to argue.

"So many?" Lilah inquired, and Celie could tell that her sister was trying to play along. "I do hope the Castle will be able to make room. We already have so many relations and other royal guests coming."

That certainly wasn't a lie, Celie thought. They did have a large number of cousins, and there were sure to be other countries sending delegations, anxious to hear the outcome of Sergeant Avery's search.

"Please ask the Castle to do its best," Rolf said to Celie.

"I had better get started right away then," Celie said with mock seriousness. She curtsied to the two men, and then to Rolf, and they all bowed back.

"I had better assist her," Lilah said, and also curtsied to everyone. She and Pogue followed Celie out of the throne room.

Celie waited until they had gotten a little way down the hall before she asked what had been going on. She had a little inkling that something about the two ambassadors had not been quite right, but she wasn't sure what.

"They're trying to take over the Castle," Lilah hissed. "But let's wait until we get to my room to explain."

"Is your room up there?" Pogue looked doubtfully at the spiraling staircase they had now passed twice. "I think this is the same staircase that was back there." He had encountered the Castle's foibles and changes many times, of course, but was not half as skilled at navigating them as the royal family.

"My room should be right here," Lilah said, frowning.

"It keeps showing me this room," Celie said, pointing up the stairs to the Spyglass Tower. "I'm starting to wonder if it's important."

Lilah looked at Celie for a moment. "Do you think so?" She was very serious: everyone knew that Celie was by far the best at interpreting the Castle's changes.

"It doesn't seem to have any real uses now," Celie told her. "But every day the Castle sends me up there at least once."

"We'd better go look," Lilah said.

All three went up the stairs, and Celie showed Lilah and Pogue the spyglasses, the book, and the dry biscuits. Pogue was very interested in the spyglasses, but Lilah flipped through the book and then shuddered.

"I hope these things don't come in handy," she said. "I've never been that keen on learning languages. You do realize that this is a Vhervhish phrase book, don't you? That's worrisome."

"What is going on with the ambassadors?" Celie asked.

Lilah and Pogue looked at each other, and Celie folded her arms tightly. It was one of those grown-up looks that said they were going to try to sugarcoat what came next.

"You see, dearest," Lilah began, but Pogue tapped her arm and shook his head.

"Celie," he said, when Lilah gave him another one of the looks. "Rolf is very young. Too young, some people think, to be the king. Not to mention that he doesn't want to be the king, at least not yet."

"I know that," Celie said, but not rudely. She was glad that Pogue, at least, was treating her like she was old enough to understand what was happening. "We need to find out where Mum—Mother and Father are first, anyway."

"True," Pogue agreed. "But it means that Sleyne doesn't have a king right now," he went on. "Your father is . . . missing." He stopped and cleared his throat. "And Rolf can't be crowned until we find out what happened to your parents. So the kingdoms around Sleyne are watching very carefully, thinking that we may be weak. Because if we are, it would be the perfect time to . . . take over."

Celie stared at Pogue, then Lilah, who nodded slowly. "So the Vhervhish ambassador is here to *invade*? But there's only one of him!"

"He's not invading yet," Lilah said. "For now he's just spying." She wrinkled her nose in distaste. "He's finding out if Rolf is smart enough, and old enough, to be a good king. And I'm sure that he's trying to pave the way for his prince to come, with loads and loads of soldiers as an 'honor guard,' so that they can attack when we're at our lowest."

"What about the Grathians?" Celie asked.

"It's the same thing," Lilah said. "Only, I think the Grathians know more about the Castle. Their ambassador is paying a lot of attention to the Castle itself. He looks around when he talks, like he's talking to the walls and not to Rolf. He must know that the Castle chooses its own rulers, and is trying to impress it."

"But hasn't the Castle already chosen Rolf?" Celie protested.

"We know that, but they don't," Lilah said grimly. "Or they don't really believe it, or they want the Castle to change its mind. The Vhervhish will probably try to take it by force, if they try at all, and the Grathians by guile."

Celie just shook her head. "It won't work," she said. "Castle Glower finds a way to get rid of *chambermaids* it doesn't like. It isn't going to sit there and let a new king take over."

"Not a lot of people, outside of these walls, truly believe

that the Castle does these things," Pogue said. "I wouldn't, if I wasn't here all the time. I've seen it stretch the hallways, and I've seen the new rooms the day they appear. But most people, even in the village, think that it's just a lot of nonsense."

Celie put her hands on her hips. "Well, they'll find out soon enough!"

Chapter 6

⁓

But the Castle didn't do anything to show its temper over the next few days. The next morning, when Celie awoke, they found exactly enough guest rooms, barracks, and stables to house precisely the number of foreign guests they were expecting. No one saw it happen, and the rooms were so perfectly normal, the stalls and barracks so perfectly plain and even worn-looking, that Celie herself had trouble believing that they hadn't been there all along.

It was a theory of her older brother Bran's that the rooms really were there all the time, they just couldn't see them. Or they were being kept in some sort of magic pocket, although Celie had never quite understood this explanation. Because the "new" rooms the Castle would produce from time to time were never that new, but appeared to be the same age as the other rooms, just a little disused. When the hallways grew, the stone flags were always worn in the middle, the walls had occasional chips or marks on them; even the tapestries appeared to be part of the same series.

"It's probably one vast structure; it might even be the size of the entire valley," Bran would say, waving his arms. "But we can only see part of it. Or it tucks the unused rooms and bits of corridor away until it wants them, in an enchanted pocket. Or it hides them on another plane of existence."

This was one of the reasons that Bran had gone to the College of Wizardry. He was always saying things like this.

Or he used to.

Celie sighed heavily as she made her way to the kitchens. She was taking the regular corridor, and not jumping out a window, because she had on her new gown, and Lilah had threatened to stuff her up a chimney with her own two hands if Celie got it dirty.

As though she would go climbing out of windows, or visit the stables, or explore a dusty attic today.

It was the day of their parents' and Bran's memorial service, and everyone was in a somber mood, waiting for the ceremony to begin. Celie wasn't in the mood to do anything that might get her dirty, and Lilah knew it, but she said it anyway because she was upset. And because she was upset, too, and because she knew Lilah hadn't meant it to be mean, Celie didn't protest or complain.

Sergeant Avery had returned from his search two days before, his face set in grim lines. He had found the torn remains of Queen Celina's traveling gown and her ruby-studded wedding band in the thicket at the side of the road. He hadn't wanted to speak further in front of Celie, but Rolf had gruffly insisted that he continue. There had been signs of further struggle, and bloodstains on the hard-packed dirt to the side of the road, the soldier had reported as he handed Lilah their mother's ring. Bodies had been found, but he couldn't say whom they belonged to, though he was reluctantly convinced that they were those of King Glower and Bran.

Celie didn't remember anything else. She had woken up in her bed this morning with a dull headache to find Lilah in full frenzy and the memorial service for those killed in the ambush converted into a state funeral for King Glower the Seventy-ninth, Queen Celina, and Prince Bran.

Their family.

Lilah seemed braced for Celie to make a fuss, but instead Celie had quietly put on her new black gown, which felt very stiff and grown-up with a royal purple sash, and did all the errands that Lilah sent her to do as quickly as she could without running. She checked with the housekeeper that the newly added rooms had linens and basins and chamber pots and everything else the guests would need. She sent a footman to the stables and barracks, and took his report back to Lilah. Now she was on her way to the kitchens, to make sure that Cook had everything she needed for the feast that night.

In Sleyne, funerals were always held at sundown, with a feast afterward that sometimes went on until dawn, so many of the guests had not yet arrived. It was only noon, after all, and there was plenty of time for the various princes and their entourages to arrive, settle in, and change before the ceremony.

"Good afternoon, Princess Cecelia," said a very subdued undercook as she entered the enormous kitchen.

The rest of the staff echoed his greeting, a ripple of quiet preceding her across the room as she made her way to the far end, where Cook was overseeing the roasting of a huge pig in the largest fireplace. A motherly woman nearly as broad as she was tall, Cook just nodded as she ladled some sort of sauce over the sizzling meat. The sauce smelled like oranges, and Celie's mouth watered in spite of her resolution to behave with decorum. She had planned on eating lunch in the kitchen after she spoke to Cook, but if everyone was going to stare at her like this, perhaps she should take a tray somewhere else.

The roasting pig thoroughly basted, Cook admonished the spit boy to keep his cranking slow and steady, and turned to Celie.

"Princess," she said.

"Cook," Celie replied.

They smiled palely at each other.

"A message?"

"Indeed."

Celie took a note out of her sleeve, not the least bit put off by Cook's short, clipped words. She always spoke this way, and it was never a sign of ill temper or impatience. Rolf speculated that her head was so full of recipes, and cooking times, and remembering when she had put the potatoes on to boil, that there was no room for fancy speech. Celie didn't mind: there was no finer cook in all of Sleyne, and perhaps the whole world.

Celie looked at her list of questions.

"Do you have everything you need for the feast?"

"Yes."

"Do you have the numbers of people who are expected to attend?"

"Yes."

"We expect to have one hundred guests staying with us for the next week after the . . . service."

"Fine."

"Prince Lulath of Grath does not eat meat," Celie went on. "Do we have a variety of non-meat dishes we can offer him?"

"Of course."

"Also, Prince Lulath's dogs require their meat to be lightly grill—"

"No."

"Beg pardon?"

"I don't deal with dogs," Cook said, her voice as impassioned as Celie had ever heard it. "I cook for people, not dogs. Talk to the kennel master."

"But they're not hunting hounds," Celie protested. "His Highness has three small—"

"Princess," Cook interrupted her. "Stand up straight!"

Celie stood up straight.

"Princess Delilah sent you to ask questions that we all know the answers to because she is grieving, but this is enough. When Prince Lulath comes with his herd of lapdogs, one of you must look him in the eye and tell him to take them to the kennel!"

"But it—" Celie protested.

"Befouling Castle Glower with hair and dirt and . . . soil from those little yappers! And during a time of mourning, too!"

Celie was rather fond of small dogs, or dogs of any kind, but she had to admit that the prince's demands seemed rather pushy, especially since he had invited himself to the ceremony. Rolf and Lilah were still worried that the Grathians would try to take over the Castle, and the list of "necessities" that had been sent ahead of the prince's traveling party seemed to confirm their fears. He was requiring that he and his men be put in the best possible quarters, and for an indeterminate length of time. He had requested special foods brought to him and his servants and dogs, a tailor on hand to help him if he needed to alter his clothes or order new ones, a carpenter in case his rooms were not to his liking, and a private study large enough for him to meet with his ambassador and other confidants as often as necessary.

"Princess Cecelia?"

Celie folded the paper and put it in her sleeve again. "I'll do it," she told Cook. "And I'll let Lilah know that you've got everything ready in the kitchen, like I knew you would."

"Thank you, Princess," Cook said.

The big woman turned to one of the kitchen maids. "Lunch, on a tray," she barked. "For Prince Rolf and Princess Delilah as well."

"Oh, and Pogue," Celie put in. "Pogue is helping Rolf."

Cook raised her eyebrows, but merely said, "Of course."

"I'll take the tray to Prince Rolf and Master Parry," one of the maids offered. She giggled, and shared a look with her friend.

"You." Cook pointed to another maid, who had been quietly ladling soup into four bowls. "Take the tray to Prince Rolf and Master Parry. You"—she pointed to the giggling maid—"Princess Cecelia and Princess Delilah.

"Now."

Chapter 7

With the maids behind her, one looking smug and the other angry, Celie wound her way back through the Castle to the small family dining room, where Rolf and Lilah had taken to barricading themselves when they needed to talk. Lilah was there now, bent over a wax tablet on which she and Ma'am Housekeeper were making seating arrangements for the feast.

"Lilah, we've brought lunch," Celie announced. "And everything in the kitchen is just fine. Cook is prepared for anything."

Celie sat down and nodded to the maid to put her tray down. She thought she'd be too nervous and upset to eat on the day of the memorial, even before it had become a funeral for her parents, and at breakfast the odor of the eggs and sausage had turned her stomach and sent her scurrying from the room. But now she practically grabbed the lunch tray out of the maid's hands without waiting for Lilah to even look up.

"I'll eat in a moment," Lilah said absently.

"You'd best eat now," Ma'am Housekeeper said. She scooped up the wax tablet. "It looks well enough, Your Highness. I'll review it one last time, and show Master Denning." Master Denning was the head butler. "We'll make any changes we think necessary, but I don't think there will be any."

"Are you sure?"

"Quite sure, Your Highness," the housekeeper said in her kind voice.

She marched out, shooing the kitchen maids in front of her, and Lilah sat down with a sigh.

Lilah lifted the lid of her tray, wrinkled her nose, and put the lid back. Celie raised her eyebrows: lunch was an excellent cheese and cauliflower soup, with bacon and tomato sandwiches to dip in it, and bunches of enormous grapes. Lilah loved cheese and cauliflower soup and grapes.

"You need to eat," Celie said sternly, taking a big bite of her own sandwich to encourage her sister.

"Yes, you do," Pogue agreed, coming into the room with Rolf.

They sat down, took the lids off their trays, and began to eat without any further greeting. Pogue seemed to be magically able to put half a sandwich into his mouth at once, without looking greedy or having anything fall out, and managed to wink at Celie at the same time. Rolf tore his sandwich into quarters, and proceeded to dunk each quarter in soup and then throw it into his mouth as though he were starving.

"We've been up since dawn," Rolf said, looking apologetic, when he'd finished his sandwich and picked up his spoon.

"Well, so have I!" Lilah's voice was shrill. "I've been running the entire Castle, you know! Getting ready for the ceremony, making sure all the guests have a place to sleep and enough food, and it just goes on and on, without anyone to help me!"

Celie would have pointed out that she had been helping, was in fact the one who had found out if there was enough food, but decided that it wasn't worth the argument.

"What about Celie?" Pogue smiled at Celie. "I'm sure she's helping."

Celie glowed and smiled back, but Lilah's dark expression smothered the smile.

"So it's just the two of us? Celie and I are expected to do everything?" Lilah was almost in tears.

"Lilah!" Rolf put down his spoon. "Stop that at once! You know that Pogue and I have been busy! He's been talking to the captain of the guards . . ." Rolf looked askance at Celie. "You know, just in case there's any unpleasantness."

"You mean, if the Grathians try to take over?" Celie raised her eyebrows and tried to look grown-up.

"Er. Yes," Rolf admitted. "And Pogue's been directing the Castle guards' move from the large barracks to other quarters to accommodate the guests' men-at-arms. And added to that, he's also kept a watch on the roads to see who's arriving."

"And what have you been doing?" Lilah did not look at all mollified.

"I have been trying to keep our family in possession of this Castle," Rolf said quietly. "As much as anyone can be in possession of Castle Glower."

Celie stopped eating. They all stared at Rolf, except for Pogue, who looked uncomfortable. He put down his spoon, too, as Lilah pushed her tray away.

"Oh, Rolf . . . you don't really think? But your room is still near the throne room! Isn't it?" Lilah's voice faltered. "Doesn't the Castle still want you to be king?"

"I assume so," Rolf said. "My room is still as it always was. But that doesn't mean anything to Vhervhine. Or Grath. It barely means anything to Father's own Council!"

"The Council?" Lilah's brow clouded. "But they support you . . . they have to, or they'll end up trapped in their own rooms or spit out a chimney, and they know it!"

"Lilah," Pogue said softly. "Rolf's room hasn't changed. At all."

"I know that, Pogue," Lilah snapped. "Rolf just said . . . Oh!"

"What? What is it?" Celie looked anxiously around.

"My room hasn't changed, Cel," Rolf repeated. "It's not any bigger. It doesn't have any royal seal on the wall, like Father and Mother's room does. There's no padded stand for the crown, or room in the wardrobe for any robes of state. I'm still just the crown prince."

Lilah looked at Rolf and spoke slowly, as though not sure what to say. "You're still the crown prince. That means that the Castle hasn't chosen anyone else to be king, right?"

A burst of hope was fluttering in Celie's rib cage like a little bird. "I know what it means!" She bounced in her seat in excitement. "I know what it means!"

"What does it mean, Celie?" Rolf turned to her, looking relieved that she might have an answer, since he apparently did not.

"It means that Father isn't dead!" Celie blurted out.

"What? No, Celie!" Lilah reached across the table and took her hand gently. "Dearest, you heard what Avery said, and what the search party found—"

"But if Father were dead, then Rolf would be the new king," Celie argued. "And since Rolf is still the crown prince, then Father must still be alive!"

"What if the Castle *has* chosen someone else?" Pogue asked suddenly. "Well . . . there's always that chance, isn't there?" He ducked his head. "Sorry, Rolf," he muttered.

Celie gave him a withering look. "But then Rolf wouldn't be the crown prince," Celie pointed out. "His room would have moved, or been made smaller, or something."

"Mother and Father's room is the same . . . isn't it?" Lilah stood up.

"I haven't looked," Rolf said slowly. He got up, too.

Now they were all on their feet, and Celie's heart was

fluttering worse than before. She couldn't believe that she hadn't checked in her parents' room before. But the Castle had been in mourning . . . hadn't it? It had draped itself in black, had refrained from making any big changes. But was that only because they were sad and scared? Did it understand death? Could it really sense what had happened to her parents, leagues away?

Pogue asked the same questions as they hurried along the corridors.

"It's a castle . . . I mean, how much could it really understand?"

"Don't talk like that," Celie warned. "It might throw you out!"

"Good question, though," Rolf said as they reached their parents' chambers. "No one really knows. But whether or not our parents are truly dead, the Castle is upset, and it's getting ready for *something*. Don't you think, Celie?"

Celie just nodded, a little out of breath from keeping up with their longer legs. The Castle was getting ready for something: the memorial service, a coronation, she wasn't sure. There was a kind of hum to the stones, a sense of awareness that hadn't been there before. Or not quite, anyway.

"Moment of truth," Rolf said, putting one hand on the latch of their parents' bedchamber.

"Please hurry, Rolf," Lilah said. "Before one of the servants sees and thinks we've run mad with grief."

Rolf opened the door, and they all pushed inside. He closed it swiftly behind them, and they looked around in the dimness. The fire and candles had not been lit, and the curtains were drawn. Celie tried to cross the room to open them, and barked her shin on a low stool.

"Ouch!"

"I'll do it," Lilah said, and gracefully made her way to the windows without bumping into anything, and pulled the heavy curtains wide.

Celie gazed around with her brother and sister and their friend. There was the bearskin rug before the hearth. There on the mantel were the ivory miniatures of all four of the royal children. The purple coverlet. Their mother's embroidery frame with a half-finished design stretched across it. The carved pedestal with the scarlet cushion on top, bearing the crown of state. Their father had taken a smaller circlet to wear at Bran's advancement to wizard.

"It's just the same," Celie whispered, and felt tears pour down her cheeks.

"Oh, what shall we do?" Lilah said, wringing her hands.

"What do you mean? This is glorious news!" Rolf's eyes were shining, and he put an arm around Celie and gave her a tight squeeze.

"We have two hundred guests arriving today for a *funeral*," Lilah reminded her brother. "What are we to do with them? Send them home? Because the Castle thinks Mother and Father are still alive?"

"Lilah!" Celie shrugged off her brother's arm, angry. "Don't you believe that they're alive?"

"I—I would like to," Lilah said, her large eyes wet with

unshed tears. "But there's also Avery's report!" She held out her right hand, showing them their mother's wedding ring on her middle finger. "And I have to be the practical one. If they're not—"

Celie rushed to Lilah and embraced her, and Rolf followed, wrapping his arms around both sisters. Pogue stood with his hands in his pockets, gazing out the window, and then finally spoke after a few minutes.

"Here's what we'll do," he said. "We'll have the ceremony; it's all been planned. The guests are arriving, and they're expecting it, and we need to honor those who we know for certain died in the ambush. Then, after the ceremony, I'll take some men up to the pass and look around myself. Quietly. I know the land pretty well, and most of the shepherds and farmers know me; they might talk to me when they wouldn't to a soldier."

"I've got a better idea," Rolf said, dropping his arms and taking up a thoughtful pose by the fireplace. "What if you went through the pass and *beyond*?"

"Where?" Pogue and Lilah asked at the same time.

Pogue winked at her, and Lilah flushed.

"To the College of Wizardry," Rolf said excitedly. "I can't believe we didn't think of this before! There must be something they can do, to verify who died, or search for any survivors with magic!"

"They must know how to track Bran," Celie said, clutching at the neck of her gown to try to contain her racing heart. "He was there for three years! Perhaps they could look for him in a—a crystal ball or something!"

"Pogue, would you?" Lilah reached out a beseeching hand to him.

He took it and kissed it, his old flirtatious ways surfacing. "For you, anything!"

Celie and Rolf rolled their eyes, but they were grinning broadly.

Chapter
8

The memorial service had taken place more than a week ago, but many of the guests still lingered at the Castle. Celie couldn't find a single corner of the Castle that didn't have some Vhervhish servant or Grathian courtier in it. They were everywhere, waving scented handkerchiefs (the Grathians) or glaring and fingering their belt knives (the Vhervhish). Plus there were the people of Sleyne, who were taking an avid interest in the "poor royal orphans." Women from the village and from every farm for leagues around kept flinging themselves at Celie, pinching her cheeks and asking if she was eating enough. Celie was trying to distract herself from the uncertainty of her parents' fate by working on her atlas of the Castle; having her cheeks pinched by a plump farmwife or her nose tickled by a wafting kerchief was not helping at all.

Celie had convinced herself that making an atlas of the

Castle would make everything all right. She envisioned finishing the final map, tidying it all up, and putting it into a leather cover. And then, just as she was tying the thong to hold the cover closed, there would be the sound of horses in the courtyard, and voices raised in excitement, and Daddy and Mummy and Bran would be there, tired but whole, dismounting from their horses. And she would hug them tightly, and then present her father with the atlas, and tell him that she had always known they would be all right, so she'd been busy working on the atlas while they were gone. And her father would praise her skill and admire the atlas, and then they would all go in to a celebratory feast.

She tried to keep this scenario firmly in her mind, but sometimes doubts crept in. Images of a grim line of wizards entering the courtyard, escorted by Pogue, to shake their heads and say that they were certain the king and queen were dead. If her thoughts turned to this ugliness, her fingers would go numb, and she would sit paralyzed for hours, staring at nothing. Sometimes when she shook off the bleak pictures in her head, she found that her cheeks were wet and her bodice soaked, but couldn't remember when she had started crying or how long it had been.

She'd started hiding under the throne again, even though Rolf never sat on it anymore. In fact, the throne room was hardly used at all, making it perfect for her to use. She would sneak into the room after breakfast and sit on the floor behind the throne. If anyone did come in, she would grab her things and slide backward into the space beneath the seat, like a turtle going into its shell.

She was drawing what she remembered of the south wing, the one where the Grathian guests were staying, when someone opened the throne room door. Celie snatched up her charcoal pencils and parchment and slithered under the throne with a sigh of annoyance. It wasn't that what she was doing was wrong; it's just that no one seemed to want her to have the time to do it.

She was about to poke her head out and scowl at whoever it was when someone spoke. Celie had been expecting Rolf's voice, or perhaps Lilah's, or maybe one of her father's Councilors. But she didn't recognize the voice at all.

And he was speaking Vhervhish.

She wiggled around until she could peep out of the latticework at the front of the throne and see who it was. There were two men: the Vhervhish ambassador and the prince, Khelsh. Khelsh was the one speaking, snarling his words and clutching at his wide belt like he might strangle the ambassador if he let go of it. The ambassador cowered before the prince's wrath, and no wonder: Prince Khelsh was built like an ox and could have picked the ambassador up with one hand if he'd wanted to.

The ambassador's reply came out in a whine. He was wringing his hands and gesturing around the throne room. He clearly wasn't happy with what he had to tell the prince, and the prince wasn't happy with what he was hearing, either. Celie heard them use the same words over and over, and she wrote them down as best she could. It occurred to her that she could look them up later in the Vhervhish phrase book in the Spyglass Tower and perhaps get an inkling about why Khelsh was so upset. The veins in his neck bulged alarmingly, and he was starting to swell like a bullfrog. Celie half expected the high collar of his thick Vhervhish tunic to pop open with the force of the prince's displeasure.

As soon as Khelsh and his ambassador left, Celie crawled out from under the throne and hurried down the servants' passage. She came out in the main corridor, and right there in front of her was the staircase that led to the Spyglass Tower. She looked around to make sure that no one saw her before she hurried up the stairs. It was the one other place where she could find privacy, but she always hesitated to go up there. It was cold, with the four enormous windows, and no rugs or tapestries to warm the stone floor or walls, and there was something . . . strange about it. There was an expectant feeling, like the Castle had put the room there for a reason, but the reason wasn't yet known.

Celie closed the big wooden door behind her, although she doubted anyone could have followed her. Even Rolf and Lilah could never find the stairway unless Celie was with them. She went over to the big table and picked up the Vhervhish phrase book. There was a list of words at the back, and she scanned through it to find the ones she had heard. She'd spelled them all wrong, but by saying them aloud she managed to find three of the words.

Castle—not surprising.

Heir, or crown prince—again, not all that surprising. Of course they would be talking about Rolf.

Kill.

That was not a good word. In fact, Vhervhish was a very warlike language, and the Vhervhish people had a number of different words for violent acts. According to the book, this particular word meant to kill in secret, or "an assassination."

Were the Vhervhish planning to assassinate Rolf?

Celie ran down the stairs, then whirled around and went back up. She gathered the book and her atlas, both for proof and in case she needed some of the other maps. Lilah had said she was going to check in the storerooms with Ma'am Housekeeper, to make certain they had enough food and candles to keep up with the continuing guests. Rolf had gone to the village to talk to the local artisans about erecting a memorial for those who had died in the ambush. Pogue's father, Dammen Parry, would be there. Like Prince Khelsh, Master Parry was the size of an ox, but unlike Khelsh, Master Parry was extremely fond of Rolf. There was no way Rolf would come to harm with the blacksmith at his side.

Whipping around a sharp turn just before the winding stair to the storerooms, Celie smacked into someone. Her atlas and the book went flying, and so did a very small dog.

"Oof! Sorry!" Celie scrambled to pick up her things,

while not one but three little dogs went yapping around her ankles. "Stop that!" She snapped her fingers at one of them when it tried to chew on her atlas.

"I am that much sorry, Princess Cecelia," said the person she'd smacked into.

She looked up, and up and up, into the face of Prince Lulath. He was very tall, but so thin he looked like one of the reeds down by the river, the kind that bent all the way to the ground when the wind blew. He was wearing a yellow tunic with sleeves that nearly brushed the ground, and his hair was almost as long as hers.

"It's all right," she mumbled.

She had a flash of fear that maybe he wanted to assassinate Rolf, too. She hid the Vhervhish book and the atlas behind her back, and started to sidle past him.

"And you are going to have so much fun today?"

"Er, I suppose," she said, taken aback. How much fun was she supposed to have, when her parents and brother were presumed dead?

"The Castle, it makes many fun things for you?" Lulath took a step to follow her as she slithered down the corridor, scooping to pick up the dogs without looking down. He was smiling broadly, his blue eyes fixed on her face.

"Sometimes. Not lately," she said.

He wrinkled his brow and nodded. "Yes, the parents. I am very much of sad for you."

"Thank you."

"I stay, because maybe you and the brother and the sister will need help," he said eagerly. "I have many years my father helped, with the Grath ruling."

"That is very nice, and I'm sure you're very good . . . at that," Celie said.

"I am not so good as you, at the talking with the Castle," he said.

Celie straightened, thrusting out her chin. Was he in league with Prince Khelsh? "No, of course not," she said with as much confidence as she could muster. "The Castle does favor me." She stroked a hand on the stone wall of the corridor. "Me and Lilah and Rolf. The Castle picked Rolf, you know, to be the next king. It will be very angry if he isn't."

"I understand," Prince Lulath said. He shifted his dogs around so that he had a hand free, and touched the wall, too. "The Castle, if it likes you, must be the very great thing."

"Yes, and very powerful," Celie said pointedly.

"That is the true," Prince Lulath said. "I have already the thanks given, that the rooms we stay in have been nice and more nice."

"Nice and more nice?" Celie stopped in the process of sidling away, hooked by what he said.

"Yes," Prince Lulath said. "They were nice when we come up here last week," he added hastily. "But now that they are bigger and . . . softer . . . they are the more nice. And here is the thanks to you, if it was you who make it to be so." He gave her a bow.

"You . . . you're welcome," Celie said. She bobbed her head. "I really must go. I have to help Lilah."

"You will thank her, also?"

Prince Lulath's head bobbed up and down, and he smiled in a way that was . . . anxious, she realized. He certainly didn't look like an assassin, standing there in his yellow tunic holding those ridiculously small dogs.

"Yes," Celie said. "Good-bye!" And she clattered down the winding stairs to the storage rooms.

By the time she found Lilah and the housekeeper, her head was so awhirl that she didn't know what to say. They looked at her quizzically as she stood in the doorway, panting (there were a lot of stairs down, and a very long corridor, before one reached the storerooms, which were probably dungeons in other castles).

"Well, what is it, Celie?" Lilah rubbed a smudge of dust off her hand.

"Have you seen Prince Lulath's rooms?" was the first thing out of her mouth, and she silently cursed herself. Rolf! She wanted to warn Lilah about Rolf being in danger!

"Of course not!" Lilah blushed, and gave Ma'am Housekeeper an embarrassed look.

"He said his rooms are nicer now than when he first came," Celie said. It occurred to her that she probably shouldn't blurt out the Vhervhish plot in front of the servants.

"Are they?" Lilah was looking over some casks of pickles. "And you came all the way down to tell me that? He has dozens of servants, Celie, they probably brought their own furnishings."

"Yes, but that wasn't the only reason why I came." She darted her eyes to Ma'am Housekeeper and then made a face at Lilah.

Celie trusted the brusque and efficient woman, and knew that she would never intentionally harm Rolf or any of their family. But there was always gossip, which spread like hot honey among the housekeeping staff. And if Prince Khelsh found out that they suspected him, would it chase him away, or would it make him act more quickly?

"Well, what is it?" Lilah rubbed at another smudge.

"I—I need to talk to you. Um, alone." She gave Ma'am Housekeeper an apologetic look.

"It's all right, Princess Delilah," the older woman said pleasantly. "We're nearly done, and there's no need for you to stay down here in the dark all day. I'll take care of the things we've talked about."

"All right," Lilah said, but she was still frowning.

"I'm sorry you're always so busy," Celie said as she and Lilah walked out of the storeroom together.

"Someone has to be," Lilah said with a little sigh. She summoned a smile for Celie. "Now, what is this all about? Why are you carrying all those books and things?"

"Oh. Lilah!" Celie stopped in the middle of the long corridor. "Lilah, it's awful! I was in the throne room, and Prince Khelsh came in with his ambassador, and they were yelling, and so I hid and wrote down what they said and

I'm pretty sure they're going to kill Rolf!" She ended in a sob.

"What? Oh, Celie! That's impossible! How did you even know what they were saying? Prince Khelsh barely speaks Sleynth."

Celie held out the Vhervhish phrase book. "This was in the Spyglass Tower," she reminded her sister. "I wrote down the words they kept repeating, so that I could look them up. But they said 'heir,' like heir to the throne, and they said a word that means assassinate." She hiccupped.

Gravely, Lilah looked at the words Celie had scribbled on her spare paper, and then she looked in the book herself. In the guttering torchlight, her face went very pale.

"We'd better go find Rolf," she said. "And Sergeant Avery."

Chapter
9

But when they did find Rolf, he didn't think there was anything to worry about.

"The Vhervhish are always plotting to assassinate someone," he said airily. "Me today, Lulath tomorrow, I'm sure."

"And Lulath is another problem," Lilah said. "He said to Celie that his rooms are nicer than when he first came."

Celie gaped at Lilah. Only a few minutes before, her older sister had brushed aside Celie's concerns about Lulath like they didn't even matter.

But before Celie could raise a fuss, Lilah gave her an apologetic look. "Now that I've had a minute to think about it, it does sound strange that Lulath's rooms would be nicer. We should look into it. But we can't very well barge into his rooms and demand to look around!" She turned to Rolf. "And how do we get Khelsh and all his men out of the Castle?"

"That should certainly be our first task," Rolf said.

"Even if you're not afraid of them trying to kill you?" Lilah's face was flushed.

Celie wasn't sure if her sister was joking or not. She very much wanted Rolf to not be afraid, to assure her that everything was all right, and that none of them needed to be afraid of anything. But on the other hand, if Rolf wasn't afraid, it might be very foolish of him. The Vhervhish were dangerous, especially Prince Khelsh, and Celie was absolutely certain that they would try to hurt Rolf before the week was out.

"Girls," Rolf said, putting an arm around each of them and steering them across the courtyard. "I promise to tell Sergeant Avery about all of this. If one of you isn't with me, then a guard will be."

"No," Lilah said, shaking off his arm and turning to go back to the guard room. "A guard should be with you all the time, even if Celie and I are there."

"Oh, all right," Rolf agreed.

Celie had been on the verge of asking him if he was afraid, since he hadn't answered the question before. But she shut her mouth now. Rolf *was* afraid, she realized with a sinking heart. Otherwise he wouldn't have turned around and followed Lilah back to the guard room.

They found Sergeant Avery and arranged for a pair of men to shadow Rolf. He also offered to have his men guard Celie and Lilah, which Rolf immediately agreed to. But Celie and Lilah exchanged looks, neither of them wanting a guard at their heels. How was Celie to slip around the Castle as she always did, with some big man following her around? And Lilah, she knew, was fond of occasionally meeting with Pogue in private.

Of course, Pogue was gone now. He had left the morning after the memorial ceremony, as promised. First he was going to question the shepherds who lived around the pass and find out if they had seen or heard anything. Then he was going on to the College of Wizardry, to find out if they had a way to track Bran. Celie was sure that he would return with important news. They just didn't know when that would be.

"I wish Pogue were here," Lilah said as they left the barracks.

"I was just thinking that!" Celie took Lilah's hand.

Rolf threw up his hands. "What is it with him? I mean, he's very good-looking, but really, both of you? And every girl in the village besides?"

"Every girl in the village besides what?" Celie said.

Lilah blushed. "Rolf! Pogue is trying to find out what happened to our brother and our parents," she reminded him. "That is all that I meant, and Celie, too, I'm sure."

"What else would I mean?" Celie gave her brother a baffled look.

"Oh, of course," Rolf said, snickering. He tugged Celie's hair. "One day, Cel, you'll look at Pogue and think, 'Never have I seen a finer specimen of young manhood!' As every other girl who has ever seen him already thinks."

"Rolf," Celie said, blushing herself as she realized what he was saying. "Are you talking about . . . kissing?"

"Yes, dear, he is," said Lilah. "But only because he thinks he's being funny. And really: he isn't." She raised her eyebrows at Rolf.

"If my jokes do not amuse you, ladies, then let me apologize," Rolf said with a show of gallantry. He bowed effusively at them, walking backward.

Celie saw Rolf's eyes flick over their shoulders, and knew that their bodyguards were following them. Immediately, her back began to itch right between her shoulder blades, and she wanted to turn around. But she shouldn't, she just knew. They were mounting the steps to the Castle's main doors now, and she could see faces peering out of the windows at them. If any of those faces were Vhervhish, she didn't want them to think that having a bodyguard was anything new and strange. Let them wonder how long the men had been shadowing the royal family. Let them see that trained fighters were always watching, waiting to leap into action to protect the Glower children.

"We should go and have a few words with Prince Lulath," said Rolf, leading them up the stairs. "Just a friendly chat. I mean, if his rooms are really that fine, it would be only polite to pop in, say hello, maybe have a little look around." He looked at Celie and Lilah to see if they agreed.

"Mother would want us to be hospitable," Lilah replied, one corner of her mouth turning up.

But they were just inside the main entrance hall when they were accosted by several of their father's Councilors. Standing silently against the pale stones of the main hall in their long black robes, they looked like a copse of trees on a moonlit night. Celie had to repress a little scream when the foremost of them moved forward suddenly and began to speak.

It was only Lord Feen, she reminded herself sternly. He had been the Speaker for the Council since before she was born . . . in fact, he had probably been the Speaker since before her father was born. His creased face was grim, but then again, it was always grim, so there was no need to assume that his news was dire.

"We have something to discuss," Lord Feen said in his quavering voice.

"Ah, Lord Feen!" Rolf made as if to slap the old man on the back, then checked himself at the last moment and merely patted him gently on the shoulder. "My sisters and I were about to pay a visit to one of our foreign guests, and then I shall be at your disposal."

"You will be at our disposal now," said the Emissary. "This is too urgent to wait upon a whim." He looked at Celie and Lilah. "The princesses are not needed," he sniffed.

"I'm staying," Celie and Lilah said together.

"My sisters are needed for whatever I am needed for," Rolf said. His voice was soft, but there was a hard edge in it that made the Emissary's eyes flash with irritation. "Shall we then, my lords?" Rolf turned and walked through the carved doors that led to the throne room.

There were three chairs in front of the dais where the throne sat. Rolf took the one in the middle, and Celie and Lilah sat on either side of him. The Councilors had to stand, but it wasn't an insult: they always did. It made them feel tall, Rolf would joke.

It made them feel more *powerful*, was Celie's thought.

The Council loomed above them now, and Celie wished that the Castle had provided taller chairs. She straightened her spine, and made sure to look Lord Feen directly in the eyes whenever he happened to glance her way. Which wasn't often, because he really only wanted to speak to Rolf. Her brother was lounging in his own chair as though bored, though Celie could see the tension in his jaw and shoulders, and knew that it was all an act to make him appear older. And braver.

It seemed to be working, Celie thought with admiration. Because Rolf didn't turn pale or flinch at what the Council had to say. He listened to them, and nodded sagely, and made thoughtful noises without really saying anything in reply, just like their father did when he was listening to something he wasn't sure he wanted to hear.

Celie and Lilah, on the other hand, both flinched *and* turned pale, and Celie had to bite her lips to keep from shouting at Lord Feen. Lilah, with her hands clenched on the arms of her chair, looked like she was trying hard not to shout as well.

Or cry.

What the Council had to say was that they felt the evidence Sergeant Avery had brought was quite clear: King Glower the Seventy-ninth was dead, and so was his queen and his oldest son. There had been a service dedicated to their memory. Now it was time for King Glower the Eightieth to take the throne.

Rolf. They wanted to crown Rolf as soon as possible.

This had made Celie and Lilah both flinch. Celie wanted to shout at them that her parents weren't dead: the Castle would have given them a sign if they were. But she had been trained not to interrupt during matters of state, or to contradict her elders, so she held her tongue. Then the rest of Lord Feen's words came clattering out, making her go paler and paler, and wanting to shout less and less, and cry more and more.

Because Lord Feen and the rest of the Council thought that the real reason Rolf was refusing the throne was because he felt incapable of ruling. The Council understood, Lord Feen kept saying, in a strange gentle voice that he probably also used with wary dogs and skittish horses. The Council would never leave Rolf to rule alone.

"Meaning what, exactly?" Rolf narrowed his eyes at Lord Feen.

"Meaning that we, your regents, will be there to guide you in every step you take, until you reach such an age that you can rule alone," Lord Feen said.

"A regency?" Lilah gasped. "But Father never would have—"

"What father, what king, ever imagines he will leave his heir alone this young?" The Emissary stepped forward. "Naturally your father didn't leave provision for a regency, because he never imagined that we would need one. But it's clear that Prince Rolf's tender age cannot support the burden of the crown."

"I see," Rolf said. He stood up. "I thank you for your concern. The kingdom needs a strong ruler, it's true, and my parents' . . . mishap . . . has been sudden and shocking. I am prepared to take the throne, and rule as King Glower the Eightieth. I have been prepared for this since I was five years old, and Castle Glower itself declared me my father's true heir. If it is indeed the will of the Council that a king ascend the throne now, before we have discovered my parents' final fate, then so be it. But no King Glower has ruled with a regency, and I do not intend to be the first!" Rolf pinned each of the Councilors with a hard look.

Celie wanted to applaud. This was why Rolf had been chosen by the Castle. He was always ready with a laugh or a joke, always willing to have fun, but when matters were serious, Rolf knew the right thing to say, and how best to say it. Lilah's cheeks were flushed, and she was looking at Rolf with admiration, too.

The Council, however, was not.

They were frowning, shaking their heads. A few of them

were smiling, but in a way that said they thought Rolf was amusing. Like a much younger child. Or a dog that could do tricks.

"That is all very well," Lord Feen said. "But you are out-voted."

"Outvoted?" Rolf frowned at Lord Feen. "What on earth do you mean?"

"The Council has put it to a vote, and agreed unani-mously that a regency is required."

"But I am also a member of the Council," Rolf said. "And I do not vote for a regency."

"Your disagreement on this matter is noted," Lord Feen said. "However, the majority is still in favor of a regency."

"But if I am king—" Rolf began.

"But you are not," the Emissary said. "Not yet. And until that time, as the crown prince, you are subject to the Council, which has decided that we shall guide your reign until you reach a more mature age."

Rolf was silent for a long time. His face was very red, and then very pale. Celie could feel her own blood rushing through her body in a strange, irregular way, and knew that her cheeks mirrored Rolf's: first red, then white, then red again.

"Very well," Rolf murmured. "If I may ask: When will I reach a more 'mature age,' as you put it?"

"The Council has decided that ten years of ruling with our wise guidance should fit you for sole rulership," the Emissary said with an oily smile. "Under our tutelage it is quite possible that you may become the greatest King Glower ever known!"

"Ten years?" Celie's throat was so dry that she could hardly whisper, and didn't think anyone heard her. "Rolf won't really be king until he's . . ."

"Twenty-four," her brother finished. "You want me to rule with a regency until I'm twenty-four." He plopped into his chair, holding out a hand to each of his sisters.

Celie took the hand offered her, reaching across the space between their chairs. Something seemed different, and that was when she noticed that the stones beneath her chair were higher, making her just a little bit taller.

Chapter 10

⸙

The coronation was to take place almost immediately. In fact, the Council had already planned the entire event, and had invited the guests from Grath and Vhervhine to stay until after it took place, which was why those princes and all their guards and servants had stayed on following the memorial. The Council had also sent invitations to other nations and to every noble in Sleyne as well.

"So the only people who didn't know I would be king by the end of the week were you two and me!" Rolf picked up one of Lilah's pillows and threw it at the wall.

"It's an insult," Lilah agreed. "But there's precious little we can do about it."

"But I'm supposed to be the king!" Another pillow smacked into the wall.

"Under a regency, that won't mean much," Lilah said.

"Lilah!" Celie found herself on the verge of tears. "Don't be mean!"

She picked up one of the fallen pillows and hugged it to her chest, huddling into a window seat and making herself as small as possible. The news that Rolf was to be a king under the thumb of a regency had been nearly as shocking and upsetting as the news of their parents' mishap, as Rolf had called it. To make it worse, Rolf had been livid for days, and he and Lilah had been arguing the entire time as well, Lilah trying to make Rolf stop complaining and accept matters, and Rolf snapping back at her and threatening to fight the Council over everything.

Lilah went to sit beside her in the window seat. "I'm not trying to be mean, dear, I'm trying to be practical. The regency will happen, and the more Rolf fights them, the more they will treat him like a child."

"So you think that I should just agree with everything they say?" Rolf picked up a pillow and looked at it like he wanted to murder it, not just toss it at the wall.

"No, I didn't say that," Lilah said. "I only mean that you should show that you are willing to work with the Council, to listen to what they have to say. It will make things a lot easier on all of us."

"I don't want things to be easy; I want them to be right!" Rolf said.

"When Pogue returns with his news," Celie began, "the Council will see that—" She stopped as Lilah and Rolf exchanged a look. "What? What's happened to Pogue?" Celie asked as her stomach dipped and lurched.

"Nothing, nothing, dear," Lilah soothed. "Or at least, nothing that we know of. But the Council sent a runner this morning to bring him back. There isn't to be any more searching for Mother and Father and Bran."

"What?" Now Celie took the pillow she'd been holding and threw it against the wall as hard as she could. It *was* very satisfying. "How could they? Isn't that . . . treason . . . or something?"

"I'm afraid not," Rolf told her. "As the Royal Council of Sleyne, they have the right to declare Mother and Father dead. Apparently." He swallowed, looking like he'd eaten something nasty. "There really is no reason, now that we've had a memorial ceremony, to spend the time and expense looking for their bodies." He held up his hands in defense as Celie gave him a murderous look. "That's what *they* are saying, not me."

"But—but we can't just give up on Mother and Father and Bran!"

"We haven't," Rolf said. He crowded into the window seat with Celie and Lilah. "I promise that we haven't. I slipped a note for Pogue to the runner, along with the official letter from the Council. I told him what has happened, with the regency and everything, and asked him to stay as long as he dared, and do as much as he can. He can say he's decided to stay in the city and visit some relatives."

"He does have cousins near the College of Wizardry," Lilah said. "If he's there now, he's probably staying with them anyway."

"You see? It will all work out just fine," Rolf said, pasting a false-looking smile on his face. "Pogue will keep going until he finds something, then he'll come back and report directly to me."

Celie knew that they were just trying to reassure her; it was clear that even Lilah and Rolf no longer believed their parents would return. But *she* still did. She knew that her father and mother and Bran were still alive. She felt it somehow. All they could do was wait and hope, and try to keep going as best they could, despite the Council, and the coronation, and all that went with it.

"Now," Rolf said, leaping to his feet. "Who wants to come to the seamstresses' quarters with me, and be fitted for some lovely, lovely coronation robes?" Rolf bowed with a flourish, gesturing for Celie and Lilah to come with him.

"I already had my fitting this morning," Celie said.

"I didn't," Lilah said, getting up and stretching. "I was down appeasing Cook. She wasn't told about the coronation, either." She took Rolf's arm, but looked back at Celie. "Do you want to come and keep us company?"

"Not really," Celie said. She saw the frown that appeared between Lilah's brows. "I'll take a bodyguard with me." Three soldiers were waiting in the corridor outside Lilah's room, ready to stalk along behind them as soon as they stepped out. Even the Council hadn't objected to the extra security measures. "I think I'll go up to the Spyglass Tower for a while."

"All right," Lilah agreed reluctantly.

"Keep a lookout for Pogue, will you?" Rolf gave her a poke in the ribs. "Make sure he doesn't dawdle on the way home."

"I will," she promised.

They stepped out into the corridor, and Rolf told the guards their plans. Two of them followed Rolf and Lilah to the right and the seamstresses' rooms, and the other tagged along after Celie, who did indeed go to the Spyglass Tower, leaving her guard at the bottom of the narrow stairs. He had twice inspected the room, and verified that it had no other exits.

When she reached the little round room, Celie cleared her throat and patted the gray stone doorway. It was smooth and cold, and yet there was a certain underlying sensation that was almost but not quite warmth.

"I don't know if you can hear me," she said hesitantly. "But Rolf is going to be crowned at the end of the week. There will be royal guests, and noble ones, coming. If you could please make some more rooms . . . or fetch them, if that's how it works. And if you could help with the coronation, I know that Rolf would really be grateful. And me and Lilah, as well. So that the regents know that you still want Rolf to be king."

A thought struck her, and she stepped forward to rest

both hands on the table. She looked around the room, a room that she suspected had been prepared for reasons she didn't understand even now. The Castle did things that they couldn't fathom, the Castle appeared to like some people and not others.

So why was Prince Khelsh still there?

And the same for Lulath and the Council. Preparations were going forward for the coronation, yet the Castle hadn't protested. Nor had it changed her parents' rooms, or Rolf's. What was going on? Was the Castle losing its powers?

The thought chilled her, and she moved to stand against one of the walls and press her face to the cold, smooth stones. She laid her palms against the stone, too, and stayed there for a long time, breathing slowly and taking comfort from the strength of the stones. She listened, too, to see if the Castle would tell her anything. When it didn't, she simply asked.

"Why don't you get rid of Khelsh? Do you like him? And do you still want Rolf to be king? Right now? Even with the Council telling him what to do?"

She listened for several minutes, but didn't hear anything. Sighing, she pushed away from the wall and glanced around. To her shock, there was an opening in the wall on the opposite side of the room. There was a black cloak folded on the table, too, made out of some sort of thick cloth she had never seen before.

Celie's whole body trembled. Had this really happened, or was she just dreaming? She touched the cloak tentatively, but it felt real, heavy and soft. What did the Castle want her to do with it? Where did the doorway lead?

She stood and fingered the cloak until a bird soaring by one of the open windows startled her. She made up her mind.

"All right, I'll do it. I trust you," she announced to the empty room.

Celie put on the cloak, which fit as though it had been made for her. She tried to see if it made her invisible, but it didn't. Or maybe she could see herself, but no one else could. The one odd thing was that it seemed to muffle any noises she made. Her feet were completely silent, there was no rustling from her gown or swish as her hair brushed her shoulders, and even her breathing seemed to be soundless now. She pulled up the hood to hide her light-colored hair, and made her way through the new entrance, down a long, winding staircase, to whatever it was the Castle wanted her to see.

The passage ended in a blank wall with a narrow horizontal opening cut into it—a peephole—at the level of Celie's eyes. She peered through, and could see a faint mesh on the other side of the wall. She reckoned that she was looking through a tapestry of some kind, but which one? There was no one in the room, and it wasn't anywhere she recognized.

It was a large room, and very impersonal. There was a round table and some high-backed chairs, tapestries on the walls, and a few small tables in the corners of the room holding candles and books and other odds and ends. Was it a new room for one of the guests? She couldn't be sure. She tried to see if any of the books were in Vhervhish, or Grathian, but they were too far away, or turned so that she couldn't read the covers.

Then the door opposite her peephole opened, and men in black robes began to file in, led by the Emissary. The Council! She was spying on the Council's privy chamber! Even Celie's father hadn't been allowed in the Council's privy chamber, and he was the king! Her heart began to pound, and she was glad that the cloak she wore muffled the noise.

She was even more grateful for the muffling cloak when Prince Khelsh entered the room, and a gasp escaped her lips before she could stop it. What was Khelsh doing there? She pressed her face as close to the wall as she could without smashing her nose, and stared through the peephole, angry and nervous and frightened at the same time.

Khelsh closed the door behind him and gestured for the Councilors to sit, acting for all the world as though he were their ruler. Celie gritted her teeth, and tried to keep quiet.

"Now you sit," said Khelsh roughly.

"Yes, thank you," the Emissary said crisply. "I agree with Prince Khelsh: let us get right to business!" He made it sound as if Khelsh's harshly accented words had been the height of courtesy. "We need to sign the agreement making His Highness the fourteenth member of the Royal Council of Sleyne, and thus a regent to Prince Rolf."

Just then the entire Castle seemed to shudder, and Celie put her palms flat on the wall in front of her, trying to soothe it despite her own anxiety.

"Shouldn't we inform His Highness first?" It was Lord Sefton, and Celie wondered if he might prove to be an ally.

"My dear Sefton," the Emissary said. "We are talking treason. Of course we aren't going to inform Prince Rolf. He'll find out after the coronation, when he has his first meeting with the full Council."

"But it's not really treason," Sefton protested. "Not when we're only trying to help Rolf rule as best he can."

Prince Khelsh and the Emissary exchanged looks, and laughed.

"That is quite enough merriment," the Emissary snapped. He had an expression of great distaste on his face. "Everyone, sign the agreement so that we can continue with the rest of our business."

"The other agreement?" Prince Khelsh's expression was cold. "You must sign also."

"For that we will need Prince Rolf's signature, once he is king," Lord Feen said.

"You did not say this before." Prince Khelsh's neck began to swell as it had before, in the throne room. He had very pale skin, like most Vhervhish, and it showed every vein and rush of blood, preventing Khelsh from ever hiding his emotions. Celie fervently wished that the blood she could see pounding through his temples would cause him to have some sort of fit.

Khelsh dipped the pen into the small ink bottle and signed with an agitated scrawl. He tossed down the pen and looked at the Emissary closely.

"But you make princeling sign, once he is king?" Khelsh asked.

"Of course we will," the Emissary said in a soothing voice. "Prince Rolf will have to agree. He'll need an heir—every king has to designate one immediately—and the Council will help him choose the heir. He's young, and naive: he'll soon realize that he's powerless to object, if he objects at all.

"And by the end of the month, my dear Prince Khelsh, you will be the crown prince of Sleyne."

Chapter
11

From now on, we may only talk freely here," Rolf said, his face so white and strained that Celie thought he might faint.

"But how will we tell each other when we need to meet here?" Celie kept folding and refolding the heavy cloak with shaking fingers.

Lilah was standing by the spyglass that faced south, nervously looking through it over and over again, adjusting the lens: searching for some sign of Pogue or their parents or anyone who could help, Celie guessed.

All three of them were in the Spyglass Tower. Celie had gathered her siblings there immediately after spying on the Council, and told them everything she had heard. They were shocked and horrified, as she was, and she was very grateful that they trusted her, and trusted the Castle. If they'd thought she was lying or telling stories to get attention, she didn't know what she would have done.

"Stick a handkerchief in your sleeve, so that a bit of it is hanging out," Lilah said.

Celie and Rolf both looked at her, a little startled by how promptly she was able to think of an answer. Lilah blushed.

"Mother told me that she and Father used to do that, when they were betrothed, and wanted to be . . . private."

"If I ever see Pogue with a handkerchief hanging out of his sleeve . . . ," Rolf threatened.

"Well, you will soon enough," Lilah said defiantly. "We'll need to let him in on this as soon as he returns." She glanced through the spyglass restlessly. "We have so few that we can trust . . ."

"There's Ma'am Housekeeper," Celie said. "I don't think she needs to know about this room, but she will help us. And Cook. Most of the servants, I think."

"And Sergeant Avery," Rolf said.

"Can we be sure?" Lilah twisted the spyglass this way and that. "Lord Feen was a Councilor to our grand-father! And the Emissary to Foreign Lands! He's always been so kind! Remember, Celie, how he brings us candy and presents when he returns from a journey?"

Celie nodded, but Rolf's lips twisted into a cynical smirk.

"That's his job, isn't it?" he pointed out. "Those presents were probably from the kings of those 'foreign lands,' and he's just taking the credit for them. I've never liked him."

"So, a handkerchief in one sleeve means we meet here," Lilah repeated, after they had all mulled over Rolf's point for a moment. "But should we drop everything and meet at once? Or should we have a special time?"

"Midnight," Rolf said decisively. "But if it needs to be sooner, put it in your left sleeve. Got it? Right sleeve, midnight; left sleeve, as soon as you can."

"But what if we can't find the staircase to the room?" Lilah took out a handkerchief, pushed it into her left sleeve, and pulled it back out again. "We could spend hours wandering. Usually only Celie can find it."

"Don't worry," Celie said. She stroked one of the walls. "Castle, we need your help. Whenever we need to meet in this room, please let Lilah, Rolf, and Pogue find it without me."

Celie wasn't sure, but she thought the stones of the wall seemed warmer under her fingers.

"I think that will do it," she said.

"Does that really work?" Rolf's eyes were wide.

"If it doesn't, we can meet in Celie's bedroom," Lilah decided. "We can usually all find that, and one of us can lead Pogue if he can't."

"That's assuming he returns in time to be of help," Rolf reminded Lilah.

"I'm sure he will," Celie said loyally.

"But until then: What shall we do?" Rolf's face was only slightly less strained.

"Don't sign the agreement," Celie said. "If you have to

name an heir, name me or Lilah. Or Lord Wellen, the Councilor of Farm Matters. He's always been so nice . . ." She trailed off, no longer certain if anyone she'd thought was nice before was a traitor or not.

"Wellen seems like a good enough sort," Rolf agreed. "And he's a second cousin, so he's got a better claim than Khelsh, who isn't even from Sleyne! At the very least, maybe I can use Wellen's name to stall for time."

"Don't act surprised when they announce Khelsh as a member of the Council," Lilah said. "Just nod like you've been expecting it."

Rolf and Celie looked at her, curious.

"It will confuse them. And probably annoy them, too," Lilah explained. "They're waiting for you to pout and act childish, Rolf. They want you to prove that you can't rule alone. But if you show everyone how gracious and . . . kingly you can be, people will question why you need regents. Khelsh isn't popular, *and* he's Vhervhish. I can't imagine people won't raise a hue and cry over his appointment. We won't have to lift a finger in protest; we'll let everyone else do it for us!" She raised a fist triumphantly.

"Then, if I start to disagree with the Council," Rolf said slowly, "in public, you know, or act shocked at what they do, people will be more likely to see my side of things."

"Yes, and when the time is right, you say that the regency is bad, that they're trying to take over the throne, or give it to Khelsh," Celie said. "By then, everyone will be ready to support you!"

"It will work," Lilah said fiercely, hugging Rolf. "It has to work!"

"How long do you think it will take?" Celie looked at her siblings, wondering how many days they would have to live under this strain.

Rolf's face became tense again, and his eyes a little wild. "Well," he said. "Let's just hope that it doesn't take ten years."

Lilah gave a hard laugh. "If it does, we'll get rid of the Council when you're old enough to be king on your own, and replace them with Councilors who aren't traitors."

"That's if they'll let me live that long," Rolf said quietly. "My guess is that once Khelsh has his feet firmly planted in Sleyne, they'll just get rid of me and crown Khelsh as King Glower the Eighty-first."

Chapter
12

Rolf Edward Daric Bryce, son of the late King Glower the Seventy-ninth, you stand before this assemblage as a supplicant," the bishop intoned. "You seek to take up the crown and scepter of the kings before you, and rule here in Castle Glower as caretaker of this magical structure, and as ruler over all of the kingdom of Sleyne."

Celie's nose itched. It was probably the incense.

She was standing behind the bishop, in a new gold satin gown, holding an incense burner. Lilah was standing beside her, also in gold satin, holding an olive branch dipped in rainwater that she had shaken over Rolf's head at the beginning of the ceremony. Celie's job was to occasionally swing the incense around and distribute the smoke, which made her cough whenever it reached her nostrils.

The bishop glared whenever she coughed, and her gown was so stiff that she swore it could stand up without her inside it, the scarlet sash so tight that she could only take little sips of air. All in all, Celie decided that it was not an auspicious beginning to Rolf's reign as King Glower the Eightieth.

Of course, he wasn't King Glower the Eightieth, not yet.

"You kneel here as one who wishes to take up the mantle of the kingship, to rule over Sleyne, and to be ruled by this goodly Castle, a thing of great and mysterious magic. Will you walk within its halls, and heed its caprices, that they may guide you to caring for your people?"

"I will," Rolf answered.

"Will you live every day for the good of Sleyne, her land, her beasts, and her people?"

"I will," Rolf said again.

The bishop waved his hand with a sour expression, and Celie hurried to swing the burner again, nearly smacking Lilah in the knee with the brass dish. She caught Rolf's eye and he winked, his lips moving in the ghost of a smile, and she grinned back, to the bishop's annoyance.

"If there is any doubt in your heart that you cannot take up the crown and scepter of Sleyne," the bishop said, coming to the end of the ceremony, "speak now!"

Rolf was supposed to say "I have no doubts." But he didn't.

Instead he raised his head and said very clearly, "If there were any doubts in my heart, the Castle would expose them. And if I were not a fit king, the Castle would have rejected me. But since it has not, I take up the crown and scepter that Castle Glower has been gracious enough to grant to me."

There was a thick silence in the hall, and Celie swung her incense burner vigorously to keep herself from cheering. The bishop had gone quickly from looking scandalized to looking thoughtful, and he took up the crown now without any hesitation, and placed it on Rolf's head. It slipped down a little—there had been no time to have a jeweler resize it—but somehow it stayed above Rolf's eyebrows and gave him a grave look. Then the bishop handed him the scepter, and Rolf kissed the jeweled knob on top and pressed it to his heart, as he'd been instructed.

"In this hall, on this day, I name you King Glower the Eightieth. Rule wisely, and well, King Glower," the bishop said solemnly.

Rolf stood, inclined his head to the bishop one more time, and then turned to face his subjects. He raised the scepter, and the assembly cheered.

Celie and Lilah cheered, too, and smiled. There were tears on Lilah's cheeks, and Celie was surprised to realize after a moment that there were tears on her own cheeks as well. It was gratifying to see how long the cheering went on, and how loud it was, with people on their feet and men throwing their caps in the air.

A pair of pages took the branch and incense from Celie and Lilah, and the girls followed Rolf down the long aisle and out into the sun of the courtyard. It was so full of people that it looked like all of Sleyne had gathered there.

People were crowding the battlements, too, and hanging out of the windows that overlooked the courtyard, and all of them had bright faces and were cheering wildly. Rolf waved and they waved back, chanting.

"What are they saying?" Lilah whispered to Celie without moving her lips, a skill Celie was bitterly jealous of.

"Eighty," Celie replied.

Indeed, everyone in the courtyard was shouting it with one voice now. "Eigh-ty, eigh-ty, eigh-ty!" It made Celie feel a bit sad, however: from now on, though the family would still call him Rolf, everyone else would know her brother as Glower the Eightieth. She wondered if he felt a little out of sorts, having his name changed. She wondered if her father had felt that way.

But if her parents returned, would Rolf go back to being Rolf? Would they have to un-king him? She supposed that Rolf wouldn't mind; it would probably be a relief. She knew that she would feel better, sleep better, once her parents returned.

"And they will," she said under her breath.

Rolf held up his hands for silence, and waited with a smile until the last cries died out.

"Thank you," he said, and the words rang clearly through the courtyard, courtesy of the Castle. "It warms my heart for my people to receive me so well." Another cheer went through the crowd. "I understand that there is a feast awaiting us just outside the gates!"

The cheers were deafening, one wordless roar. Lilah

had taken up the matter with Cook earlier in the week, who in turn had employed anyone who could turn a spit or knead bread in order to provide food for everyone who wished to attend the coronation, from Prince Lulath of Grath to the village goatherds.

"What's this?" The Emissary had stepped out from behind a gaggle of nobles. "I wasn't aware of any feast for the peasantry." He had a large, very false smile plastered across his face.

"That's quite all right," Rolf said airily. "I made arrangements with the staff some time ago."

"In the future, you will need to inform us of these little whims," the Emissary said in a patronizing voice that made Celie want to kick his shins.

Rolf gave a noncommittal nod of the head, and turned back to the cheering crowd. He raised his arms for silence again, and started to say, "Now, to the fea—" but the Emissary interrupted him.

"Excuse me, Your Majesty," he said loudly, but Celie thought that only the front rows of the crowd heard him, because the Castle didn't amplify his words the way it did Rolf's. "There is one more announcement that must be made."

He walked over to Rolf, forcing Celie to scoot out of his way. She pressed herself to Lilah's side, dreading what was coming next. They hadn't known exactly when the Council would make their announcement. Rolf had suspected it would be after the coronation, if they didn't say something before. But to do it now, when everyone was cheering for Rolf . . .

"As a member of the Royal Council of Sleyne," the Emissary said, and still the Castle didn't amplify his voice, and people whispered to each other, trying to pass along what he said and making a great rush of noise through the courtyard, "I have something to announce. It has been judged by the Council that His Highness . . . His Majesty, that is, King Glower the Eightieth, is too young to rule alone. In these uncertain times, when our beloved late King Glower the Seventy-ninth can be attacked and killed within our own borders, we need all the wisdom we can muster to guide us. Therefore, until he reaches maturity, the Royal Council shall stand as regents to King Glower. And with us, to specially tutor the king in foreign diplomacy, will be our newest member of the Council, Prince Khelsh of Vhervhine!" He said this last in a happy shout, as though expecting the assembly to cheer in excitement.

Instead there was only muttering as people passed on the news. The bright faces, alight with hope and joy, that had looked up the steps at Rolf when he emerged from the Castle, were now dark and confused as they tried to understand the reasons behind it.

"Thank you, my Lord Emissary," Rolf said, and Celie was proud of him for having only the faintest trace of bitterness in his voice. He addressed the public again. "There is much to talk about," he said, and Celie smiled as the Castle obligingly carried his words to the battlements. "But while we talk, let us feast!"

The cheers were ragged at best, and ended quickly. People dispersed, while Rolf turned around, stuck his scepter in the crook of his right arm, and held out his left to Lilah. She took it, and Celie went quickly to his right side, standing as close to him as she could without bumping into the jeweled scepter sticking out from his elbow.

"Let's take the back way to the banquet hall, sisters dear," he said. "So much shorter than winding through the crowd in the courtyard." He steered them along the apse toward the rear door of the chapel.

"Your Majesty!" The Emissary's smile was gone, now that the pages were closing the massive doors.

"Yes, my lord?" Rolf looked over his shoulder with a mild expression, but kept on walking calmly toward the back.

"There is much to discuss."

"How so?" Rolf's eyebrows touched his crown. "I have been crowned, you have made the announcement. Now we feast!"

"But . . . do you not have something to say to me?"

The Emissary, Celie realized with a bubble of laughter that she managed to bite back, was startled and perhaps even offended that Rolf wasn't angry. He had probably been waiting for Rolf to scream and argue over Prince Khelsh's appointment, but Rolf hadn't even blinked. Celie very gently squeezed Rolf's arm, just above the elbow, and he gave her a quick wink.

"Not at present," Rolf said, looking slightly baffled.

"Well . . . but . . . I rather thought you might have something to say about Prince Khelsh," the Emissary spluttered.

"Not at all," Rolf said coolly. "He's a bit of a blowhard, but really, it's what one expects of a Vhervhish royal, isn't it?"

"But . . . are you not surprised at his appointment?"

Rolf laughed. "Oh, my Lord Emissary!" He shook his head. "I've known about that for days!"

They had come to the little door at the back, the Emissary trailing behind them with a nonplussed expression, and the bishop watching from the nave. The bishop had a shrewd look on his face, and Celie gave him a cheery wave. He raised one eyebrow in reply.

"Shall we see what magnificence Cook has prepared for us?" Rolf said to Celie and Lilah. He gave the Emissary a querying look. "Are you coming this way, my lord?"

"N-no . . . I have things to see to," said the Emissary.

"Well, try not to miss the entire banquet," Rolf said. "People will talk—more than they already are, that is—if my regents are not there to show their support." He looked beyond the Emissary to the bodyguards who had followed them as well, silent and nearly unnoticeable, despite their size and the brightness of their weapons. "Come along, boys," Rolf called.

The Emissary, still looking extremely put out, had to step aside quickly as the three guards nearly pushed him aside to follow Rolf and the two princesses. Blaine, the guard assigned to Celie, saw her pleasure over this and gave her a faint smile. He took the door from Rolf.

"Lead on, Your Majesty, Your Highnesses," he said, and bowed them into the passageway with a flourish.

"Hungry, my royal sisters?" Rolf adopted a plummy voice. "We ourselves could eat a gilded ox."

"As could I, my most royal brother," Celie said.

"Let us continue on to the feast, then!"

Chapter
13

I loved the Emissary's expression so much," Celie said with a sigh of pleasure.

It was nearly dawn, and she was lying on the rug under the table in the Spyglass Tower, holding her stomach. The feast had indeed been magnificent, and her tight gown had nearly split after four hours of eating. Cook's attendants had brought out course after course, to great cheers and much admiration.

When peacocks, roasted and then bedecked with their tail feathers once again, had been brought out on gold platters, Rolf had risen to his feet, insisted that Cook be brought in, and then toasted her. She had blushed like a girl and twisted her hands in her apron. Rolf had promptly removed the feathers from the bird in front of him and given them to Cook, who curtsied and went back to the kitchen giggling. The feathers, Celie knew, were worth a gold mark each, and a very thoughtful reward for Cook's hard work. Then she and Lilah had gone with Rolf and several guards to walk among the commoners on the green in front of the Castle, nodding and smiling and sharing a drink of cider here, an iced cake there.

From everyone came endless questions about the regency.

The siblings had known it would be this way, and had already prepared a careful answer: Rolf was very young, and they were all in shock over their parents' and brother's terrible fate. It was good of the Council to take this active stance.

And that was all they would say, no matter how they were pressed. Rolf had spent the last several days formulating the answer. He wanted to be polite, and take the high ground, as they had agreed. But he also wanted to imply that it was the Council's decision, and he wanted to avoid saying that their parents and Bran were dead. It seemed to be working: the whispers and questions continued even after they heard Rolf's answer, so that the siblings knew the people were still uneasy about the regency, and still questioning it.

"The Emissary's expression?" Lilah yawned and plumped herself on one of the chairs with a lack of her customary grace.

"When Rolf said he'd known about the prince's appointment for days," Celie clarified. "The shock . . . you ruined the terrible surprise he had planned, Rolf!"

"Exactly!" Rolf laid the crown on the table and rubbed his forehead.

"That was my idea," Lilah pointed out.

"Yes, and a capital one it turned out to be!" Rolf said with enthusiasm. "I wasn't sure how to do it, but when he stepped forward and I saw that he was going to announce the regency right then and there, I decided to just plunge in. Seeing his shock was magnificent! He'll be thinking there's a spy on the Council, or a sympathizer at the very least. If we know about their moves before they make them, it will keep them off balance."

"Wonderful," Celie agreed happily.

"Yes, but while it was certainly a blow that Khelsh wasn't a surprise," Lilah said, "the trick is going to be keeping up with them. How will we know about their next moves? Will the Castle keep on showing us? Or Celie?"

"Of course it will," Celie said fondly. She patted the floor at her side. "Won't you, my only darling?" Celie was now thoroughly convinced that the Castle wasn't just magic, but a living thing, and furthermore, that it was firmly on their side.

She thought she felt a quivering beneath her hand, as though the Castle were purring.

"What do you suppose the Castle is made of?" She felt her eyelids growing heavy. It had been a very long, exciting day, and now she wanted to crawl into bed and sleep for days.

"Stone," Rolf answered. "What else would it be made of?" He reached over and flicked her shoulder. "I think it's time for you to be in bed."

Celie made a face at him. "I meant: What makes Castle Glower special? How does it do so many wonderful things? Is it alive? Was it built by a wizard?"

"People have been speculating about that for centuries," Lilah said. "But nobody has ever found out."

"I know all that . . . but I still wonder," Celie said.

"If the Castle was ever going to tell anyone its secrets, I think it would be you," Rolf said. He reached down and squeezed Celie's ankle. "Now come along, sleepy. You'd better go to bed. It's almost time for breakfast."

"Oooh, don't mention food," Celie groaned. "I might be sick."

"Pogue!" Lilah said.

"No, I'm Rolf," Rolf said, giving her a baffled look.

"No, I mean it's Pogue," Lilah said, her voice high with excitement. She had one eye pressed to the spyglass she'd been fiddling with. "And he's riding hard."

Rolf crossed the room in two strides, and Celie scrambled up from the floor.

"Are you sure?" Rolf put one hand on the spyglass, and Lilah stepped back to let him look. "It is!" He looked over the top of the brass spyglass, squinting at the road beyond the Castle. "This spyglass can see a lot farther than any I've ever used before. He's well beyond the village, even."

Lilah gave him a disgusted look. "You just got finished telling Celie that the Castle is magic and mysterious, which we all knew, and now you're impressed by a *spyglass*?" She nudged him aside and looked through it again.

"I want a look," Celie said, and Lilah grudgingly moved aside for her.

It was Pogue, but he was indeed some distance away. His horse was only just coming into the valley, yet Celie could see him quite clearly through the spyglass. He was bent low over his horse's neck and riding hard despite the dim, gray light. His horse's hide was dark with sweat, and Pogue looked muddy and travel-stained.

"Do you think he has bad news?" Celie stepped back and let Lilah look again.

"I don't know," Lilah said, sounding worried.

"Well, we'll know shortly," Rolf said easily. "He'll be here soon." He paused, squinting again. "That is, if his horse makes it: the poor beast looked ready to drop."

"Shall we ride out to meet him?" Celie gave her brother an eager look.

"By the time we had an escort, and everyone was mounted and ready to leave, he'd be at the gates," Rolf said, shaking his head. "I'm going to pop down to my room and put some clean clothes on, splash a little water on my face, and get ready to meet him at the gates. Best if you girls do the same. I don't think we'll be getting to bed any time soon."

They went down the stairs and changed into new clothes. For Celie that meant her black gown with the purple sash, which swished when she walked and made her feel quite grown-up, if a little depressed at having her first grown-up gown be one of mourning. She washed her face, and when Lilah was dressed she braided Celie's hair and pinned the braid across her head like a crown. Arm in arm they went to the courtyard, where they met Rolf.

"Just in time," he said, nodding at the main gate.

The guards were hailing someone, and after a moment they let a single horseman through. It was Pogue, on his sweating, tired horse. The animal trudged into the center of the courtyard and stopped. Legs braced wide, nostrils blowing hard, its head drooped and didn't move again.

"Pogue! Are you all right?" Lilah ran to him, with Rolf and Celie right on her heels.

Pogue looked down at Lilah with bloodshot eyes. His face was streaked with sweat and dirt, and his hair was standing on end. For a moment, he appeared to be struggling to remember her name, and he swayed in the saddle a bit.

"Delilah?" He shook himself like a dog and cleared his throat. "Lilah! Rolf!" He dismounted, seeming to gather energy from some unknown source. "They're alive!"

"What!" Lilah reeled backward, and Rolf caught her around the waist before she fell.

"Mummy and Daddy?" Celie ran to Pogue and grabbed hold of the front of his tunic. "You found Mummy and Daddy and Bran?"

"Not quite 'found,' but they're alive for certain," Pogue said, patting her awkwardly on the shoulders.

"Come inside," Rolf said in a low, urgent voice. He steadied Lilah before moving to help Pogue. "Take care of his horse," Rolf called out to the groom hovering nearby.

"Let me just tell you—"

"Not here," Rolf interrupted. "Not here. A lot has happened."

Walking so close they were stepping on one another's heels, they hurried into the Castle. The Emissary was standing there, an unctuous smile on his face, but Rolf brushed by him with a muttered apology. They made for the narrow staircase to the Spyglass Tower, and as soon as they started up the steps, the stone wall sealed behind them, cutting off the Emissary's protests.

"How did it do that?" Pogue sounded dazed. "What day is it?" He shook himself and almost turned back, but Rolf tugged his arm and kept him going up the stairs. "Can we get back out?"

"Yes, of course," Rolf assured him. "This is the only room in the Castle where we can be alone. We can usually find it, but it's easiest to come up here with Celie."

"All right," Pogue agreed, still sounding stunned.

"And if we need to meet here," Rolf went on, "put a handkerchief in your sleeve. Left for immediately, right for at midnight."

Pogue blinked rapidly. "But . . . why would we need a signal like that? Why would we need to meet here?"

They had reached the top of the steps, and Pogue collapsed on a stool, exhausted and confused. Celie and her brother and sister stood in front of him. Celie didn't want to explain everything that had happened to *them*. She wanted to hear Pogue's news at once—were their parents and Bran really alive?

"You'd better tell us your news first," Rolf said. There was a pitcher of water and a cup on the table that hadn't been there before. He poured Pogue a cupful, and when the other young man had drunk, Rolf took the cup back and rolled it between his hands. "Are they alive?"

"As far as the wizards can tell, yes," Pogue said, leaning back against the wall. "I couldn't see anything myself at the ambush site. I'm afraid that scavengers, human and animal, have picked the area clean." He grimaced. "No one nearby knew anything more than we already knew. So I went from there to the College of Wizardry. They'd heard about it, of course, but the rumor in the city is that the entire royal party had definitely been killed. So naturally it hadn't occurred to them to try to track Bran.

"I told them our suspicions, and led some wizards back to the site of the ambush," Pogue continued. "They sniffed around. Did some spells, tasted some of the dirt and the bark off the trees."

"They tasted dirt and bark?" Celie wrinkled her nose.

"That's why you won't find me at the College," Pogue said.

Lilah made an impatient noise, and Celie ducked her head. Pogue, looking chastened, went on.

"They could see which soldiers had died—I had the list you gave me—and they were right every time. They knew that Sergeant Avery got away. Then they got really excited. They said that the king, the queen, and Bran were definitely alive! They left the site of the ambush just before Avery did."

"Still alive?" Celie's heart was humming, it was beating so fast. Tears were slipping out of her eyes and she didn't realize it for a minute or two. Lilah made a little sobbing, moaning noise and put her arms around Celie.

"Alive," Lilah whispered. Then she buried her face in Celie's neck and wept.

"Where are they?" Rolf was also wet-cheeked, but he managed to stand straight and tall nonetheless.

Pogue rubbed the back of his neck. "They don't know."

"Why not?" Celie cried. "If they can tell who was there, and if they're alive or dead, why can't they follow the trail to Mummy and Daddy?" She was hugging Lilah fiercely, and didn't care if she sounded babyish when she called her parents "Mummy and Daddy."

"Because the trail ends not far from the ambush site," Pogue told her. "It just . . . disappears. They can't find a single footprint, nor locate their auras."

"But they're *wizards*!" Celie refused to accept such a silly answer. Wizards could find anything . . . wizards could *do* anything! Surely it would be easy for them to find someone's trail, particularly if it was someone they knew, like Bran. He had lived with them, trained with them, for three years!

"Bran is also a wizard," Pogue reminded her, echoing her

thoughts. "They suspect it was magic, Bran's magic, that hid the trail. The wizards think that they're in hiding."

"But what do they need to hide from?" Outraged, Celie pushed Lilah away, though not roughly. "Why don't they just come home? If there are no more bandits lurking in the forest, why hide?" Her voice broke. "We're here all alone, with the Council after us, and Prince Khelsh . . . It's been awful!"

"Maybe they know that home is dangerous now, too," Rolf said.

They all turned to look at him. Rolf was staring out one of the windows, his face gilded by the morning light, with one hand clenched in front of his chest. His mouth was a thin line, and all the jokes and teasing had gone right out of him.

"What has happened here?" Pogue sat up straight on the stool, watching Rolf carefully. "What's happened since I've been gone? Why are we meeting in a sealed room, in secret?"

"Rolf is the king," Celie blurted out. "Glower the Eight-ieth."

Pogue blinked. "I thought you were waiting for me to report back. I'm sorry it took so long, but—"

"Didn't Rolf say in his message what was going to hap-pen?" Lilah drew over two stools, and pushed Celie gently onto one while she took the other.

Rolf remained standing. "No. I only told him to return

as swiftly as possible. I didn't want the letter to be intercepted." He swung around to face Pogue. "The Council decided that I would be crowned this week . . . yesterday, that is. And that I needed a regency to guide me while I learned to be king. The Council, plus Prince Khelsh of Vhervhine, are the new regency, and I am their puppet-king until Khelsh kills me or I turn twenty-four, whichever happens first. Can you guess which one Khelsh is hoping for?"

"This is madness," Pogue said, stricken. "Can they do any of these things? Isn't there some sort of . . . precedence? Has the Castle made its will known?"

Rolf just shook his head.

"The Castle is on our side!" Celie was stung by Rolf's lack of loyalty.

"I'm not saying that it isn't, Cel," her brother quickly said. "But it also hasn't kicked the Councilors out or Khelsh—"

Pogue's eyes went wide. "But if something happens to Rolf . . ."

"We'll have a Vhervhish king," Rolf finished for him.

Chapter
14

⟨≈⟩

They thought about letting Pogue get cleaned up and into fresh clothes before braving the Council, but Rolf decided that it would look more dramatic if he was still sweaty and dusty, and Pogue agreed. He also said, with faint embarrassment, that he was afraid if he did go home for clean clothes he'd collapse from exhaustion when he saw his bed. So, with a filthy Pogue in tow, they marched into the throne room. Prince Khelsh was there, and so was the Emissary. Celie almost stuck her tongue out at them both; she was so tired of their whispering in corners and causing problems.

Rolf waved a hand at their bodyguards. "Why don't you wait out here with Prince Khelsh's guards?" The guards took up positions just outside the throne room, forcing Prince Khelsh's guards to do the same. The Vhervhish guards slunk out of the throne room with dark looks and much muttering.

Celie accidentally stepped on one of their feet on her way past, which probably hurt her more than the guard, since she was wearing thin leather slippers and he had a heavy boot on. But he gave her a startled look, and she was pleased with her little act of defiance all the same. She raised her eyebrows and the man ducked his head and apologized for being in her way.

Pogue closed the doors behind them all, and folded his arms. Though not quite as broad as his father, his pose strained his tunic at the shoulders, and the sweat-streaked dirt on his face made him look positively menacing.

"Excellent news," Rolf told the Emissary and Prince Khelsh brightly. He strode up to the dais and then took off the crown. He rested it on the seat of the throne and then turned to face the prince and the Emissary with a broad smile. "I won't be needing that anymore!"

"You are . . . give up crown, yes?" Prince Khelsh had to struggle to find the right words, but he looked very eager all the same.

"Abdicating, you mean?" Rolf shook his head. "Not hardly. But I won't need to wear the crown, or sit on the throne, *since my father is still alive.*" He put his fists to his hips and watched the Emissary and Prince Khelsh carefully, as Celie, Pogue, and Lilah did.

"Now, Your Majesty," said the Emissary with a sigh. "We've been through this. There has been a thorough search of the area, and there is no way that your parents are still alive—"

"According to the College of Wizardry, they are very

much alive," Rolf interjected smoothly. He gestured at Pogue. "Master Parry has just brought the news. They found their tracks leading away from the ambush site: Father, Mother, and Bran." Again the bright smile. "I'm about to summon Sergeant Avery and send him with a regiment to search the area again, with the help of the wizards. I'm sure that together they will be able to find my parents and brother in no time."

Prince Khelsh and the Emissary exchanged looks, and Celie clenched her fists. She knew that whatever they were about to say would sound nice on the surface, but be dripping with nastiness inside. Glancing over, she saw that Pogue's jaw was set and he also had his hands clenched. Rolf had bit the inside of his lip, and Lilah was already drawing a breath to snap back at them.

"Now, now, King Glower," the Emissary said. "There is no need to get all excited. If you wish to send a few men out on another search, then by all means do so. But as one of your regents, and I'm sure the prince here agrees with me, I don't think it's wise to raise everyone's hopes. Not to mention how vulnerable that leaves the Castle in this delicate time, if the soldiers are off beating the bushes for ghosts."

"But you aren't my regent," Rolf explained again. "I am not the king. My father is still the king, something we all should have known when the Castle kept his chambers exactly as they always were." Rolf's anger showed in the intensity of his voice, and Celie clenched her fists harder, hoping that her brother wouldn't lose his temper. It would only make the Emissary more smug, and Prince Khelsh more amused.

"You were crowned yesterday," the Emissary said, a smile on his face that was very nasty indeed, "and the prince and I and the rest of the Council were legally made your regents. If your father is still alive, why has he sent no messages, made no attempt to contact us? Rather than force the kingdom of Sleyne to wither without leadership, we have crowned you. You are the king, and the Council is here to guard your actions. And right now, two of your guardians are telling you that it is futile to persist in looking for your parents."

"Once I announce to the people that my parents are still alive, you will find that your regency is very short-lived, and your time on the Council will be over just as swiftly," Rolf said, still controlling his anger.

The Emissary stopped being oily. "And you'll find it very difficult to act like a petulant little boy when your sisters are locked up in the Hostages' Tower," he snarled.

"Go, go!" Pogue grabbed Celie and Lilah by the shoulders and pushed them back toward the door.

Celie turned to run, and there was only a large arch—the doors were gone—leaving the guards standing with startled expressions. She snatched up Lilah's hand and pulled her older sister through the arch. They darted between the guards to another arch that had opened on the far side of the main hall. It closed behind them with a crash of stone, sealing the guards out, and the sisters looked around to find themselves in Celie's room. Through another arch they could see Lilah's room, and the other way out was the narrow staircase to the Spyglass Tower.

Celie spun around, staring at the sudden changes. "How did the Castle . . . this was never . . ."

"We don't have time," Lilah panted. "Grab some of your things and get up to the Tower."

"What about Rolf and Pogue?"

"If the Castle's helping us, I'll wager it's helping them," Lilah said, hurrying through the arch into her bedroom.

Celie forced herself to stop staring and think. "I'm going to bring my pillows and blankets, too," she said.

Her stomach was a horrible, aching hole. She'd known that the Emissary was going to do something nasty. They should never have let Rolf go to the throne room. They should have just gotten horses and ridden straight to the hills to look for Mummy and Daddy themselves. Tears ran down her nose and dripped onto the bedclothes.

"Do you have anything to eat in your room?" Lilah called through the archway. "The only thing I've seen to eat in the Tower is those awful hard biscuits."

"No," Celie said, and her voice came out choked.

"What's the matter?" Lilah came to the archway, a questioning look on her face, then she saw that Celie was crying and came all the way into the room. "Celie darling, what's wrong?"

111

"When will it end?" Celie threw herself on her sister's neck. "I keep waiting and waiting for Daddy to come through the gates and stop all this . . . this nastiness from happening, but he never does! What will we do now? Isn't anyone going to help us?"

"I don't know, I don't know," Lilah said, wetting Celie's head with her own tears. "I don't know, darling."

"You're not helping, either," Celie sobbed.

"I'm sorry," Lilah said, and half laughed, half sobbed. "But listen to me," she said after a moment. She pulled away so that she could look Celie straight in the eyes. "I know that this will all turn out all right, and do you know why?"

Celie shook her head.

"Because we have something that Prince Khelsh and the Emissary don't have: the Castle. The Castle is on our side, Celie. I don't know how it's happened, or why it's happening now, but the Castle is on our side. I really think it loves you, and I feel like it loves me and Rolf and Mummy and Daddy and Bran, and even Pogue! The Castle will help us, and we will beat them!"

"Are you sure, or are you just telling me that so that I'll stop crying?" Celie asked.

"I'm sure," Lilah said, giving her a little shake. "I know that Rolf and I have been saying some things lately to make you feel better. But this isn't one of those things. I believe that the Castle can help us, and I believe that we will win. Mother and Father and Bran are alive, Celie, I know it's true now. I wasn't certain before, but now I am. We just have to hold the Castle until they get back."

"Hold the Castle?"

Lilah nodded. "It's up to us to make certain that the Council doesn't do anything more horrible to anyone. We have to make sure that Rolf and Pogue are all right. That Khelsh doesn't take over, that everything and everyone in the Castle is protected until Daddy gets back and kicks the Council out on their old, wrinkly . . . bums!"

"Lilah!" Celie put one hand to her mouth, a little shocked, and then she giggled.

"You heard me," Lilah said, with a militant light in her eye that Celie had never seen before. "Now get your things and let's get up to the Spyglass Tower."

Celie piled her pillows and folded blankets into her velvet coverlet and then tied the whole thing into an enormous bundle. She wasn't sure if the Castle was going to close the door to her room permanently once she and Lilah got to the Tower, so she just threw the bundle as far up the steps as she could. Then she went back and grabbed her old gray gown, her nightgown, some underthings, stockings, and slippers, and piled those on the stairs. She took her atlas, the Vhervhish phrase book, some paper and pens and ink; at the last minute she snatched Rufus from the back of her wardrobe.

Rufus was a stuffed cloth lion she had had since she was a baby. Rolf had started teasing her about still sleeping with Rufus when she was eight, so she had reluctantly put him in the back of the wardrobe. But she still pulled him out when no one was around and she was feeling sad or sick. He was saggy now, and sort of grayish, rather than plump and cheerfully yellow, but that was all right with Celie. She stuck him into her bundle of bedclothes just as Lilah arrived with her own things.

All of Lilah's gowns were neatly folded and wrapped in a cloak, and she was carrying her bedding in a large basket. She frowned at the mess Celie had made, but didn't say anything.

As soon as they were both on the stairs, lugging their burdens, the door to Celie's room sealed behind them. Once they got to the top, the stairs disappeared as well. The two sisters looked at each other for a moment, and Celie thought that she might cry again.

"What about Rolf and Pogue?" she asked.

"We have to trust the Castle," Lilah said simply.

She nodded, and did her best not to cry. Soon Lilah had her busy arranging her bedding on one side of the room. Lilah put her things next to Celie's, and helped her spread her gowns on top of one of the trunks against another wall.

When they turned around, another doorway had opened just beside them, making Lilah jump. It was a small dark stairway that Celie recognized as the one that led to the Council's private chamber. The sound-muffling cloak was just inside the entrance, hanging from a hook.

"Where does this go?" Lilah poked her head into the opening, and looked at the cloak suspiciously.

"The Council's privy chamber," Celie said. She reached around Lilah and plucked the cloak off the wall. "I'll go find out what's happening."

"I'd better come with you," Lilah said.

"I think you should stay," Celie said. "There's just one cloak. It makes it so you don't make any noise and can spy on people."

Now it was Lilah's turn to look near tears. "But I don't just want to sit here alone," she said.

"You could watch out the windows, and see if another search party gets sent out," Celie suggested. "That will mean that someone is actually listening to Rolf. And someone should wait to see if Rolf and Pogue make it up here."

"All right," Lilah said meekly. She sighed. "You'd think all that food we ate last night would have stayed with us longer, but I'm starving. I'll have to eat some of these hard biscuits."

"Don't eat them all, you'll break a tooth," Celie said with mock severity. She pulled on the cloak and put up the hood. She stomped her feet, but they made no noise. "Do you see?"

Lilah gaped as Celie's mouth moved, but no sound reached her. "Amazing," she said. "Now hurry!"

Celie hurried as much as she dared on the narrow, dark stairs. They seemed to go on a lot longer then she remembered from the first time. At last she came to the little slit in the wall, behind the tapestry, and peeped through.

The entire Council wasn't there, but Prince Khelsh, Lord Feen, and three others were sitting around the heavy table. The prince was sitting in an enormous chair that looked enough like a throne to make Celie grit her teeth. He was leaning back, his hands on the carved arms of the chair, a smug look on his face. The Councilors were looking at one another uneasily, and Celie guessed that Khelsh had just finished telling them what had happened that morning.

"If there's any chance that His Majesty is still alive," one of the Councilors said, "then we should certainly look for him. And the queen and prince!"

"Impossible," Khelsh said. "They are made dead, the wizards must lying be."

"But if their magic has revealed that Prince Bran, at least, is still alive, we must send someone to search," the Councilor protested. "The wizards know how to find one of their own!"

"If alive, why not here?" Prince Khelsh asked. "He could have to the Castle walked." He shrugged. "Is dead."

"You seem very sure of yourself," Lord Feen said.

"I sure? Yes!" Khelsh laughed loudly. "My best assassins did I send."

Celie let out a small scream.

Lord Feen and the other Councilors looked variously ill or outraged.

"What devilry is this?" The Councilor—it was Lord Sefton, Celie saw—was on his feet. "What have you done?"

"I make sure what I want," Prince Khelsh said. He was still slumped in the chair as though completely relaxed, but Celie could see that he was gripping the arms ever so slightly, and there was a tension to his legs that said he could leap to his feet at any moment.

"You were behind the ambush!" Sefton pointed a long, shaking finger at Prince Khelsh. "Those were your men!"

"Yes," Khelsh admitted with a shrug. "As I plan wif Emissary."

"The Emissary?" Sefton was the color of dried paste now. "And now these men continue to hunt the king and queen and their son?"

Khelsh gave the man a hard look. "You no like?"

"Not like it? You are talking about treason, and assassination!" Sefton clutched at the edge of the table as though it were the only thing keeping him upright.

"What were we talking about at the last meeting, or the one before?" the Emissary said with an expression of amusement that made Celie want to punch him until his smile went away. "But if you're feeling squeamish now . . . guards!"

Immediately two burly Vhervhish soldiers, one of them the man whose foot Celie had stepped on earlier, came into the room. "Arrest him for treason," the Emissary said, flicking a finger at Lord Sefton, whose fists were clenched, lips bloodless in shock.

The two men seized the Councilor and dragged him, shouting, from the room.

"We appear to have an opening on the Council," the

Emissary announced as soon as the door closed behind them. "Can anyone think of a likely candidate?" His voice was perfectly cool.

Khelsh grunted. "I want my cousin Khulm. Smart. But not so smart I must kill him, eh?" Khelsh didn't wait for an answer. He laughed and pushed himself to his feet. "He here, wait in room. I tell him," he said. "No others here be foolish," he warned, wagging his finger at Lord Feen as though he were a child. Laughing again, he went out of the room and slammed the door.

Celie didn't care what Lord Feen or the Emissary said after he left. They were traitors and cowards, and would probably sit there dithering and wringing their hands anyway. She pulled the cloak tight about her so that she wouldn't trip, and hurried up the stairs to tell Lilah about the terrible new thing Prince Khelsh had done.

And that they might have another ally, although this one was locked in the dungeon for the time being.

Chapter
15

It was the next morning, almost noon, before Rolf could join them. He brought some food with him, which his sisters fell upon like wolves. While they ate he told them everything that had happened to him.

"It's just as I thought it would be, only now the Emissary has come right out and said it to my face," Rolf said, staring at Lilah as she folded an enormous slice of ham and crammed it into her mouth. "I'm to be their puppet: do what they say, say what they tell me, or they'll kill me and put Khelsh on the throne."

"Won't they try to do that anyway?" Celie was eating an apple, taking the largest bites she could without choking. Juice ran down her chin onto her gown, and she didn't even try to wipe it off with a napkin.

"I don't think so—at least, not if I cooperate," Rolf said.

"The Emissary probably needs to wait until people get used to having a Vhervhish prince around. I just hope Khelsh is that patient," he said, shaking his head skeptically.

"He won't be," Celie said. "He's already replaced one member of the Council with one of his own men. He'll keep doing it until they're all Vhervhish." She shuddered.

"He's replaced someone? Who?"

Celie and Lilah told him what Celie had heard, and then Rolf told them everything else that had happened. Like the Emissary having Pogue locked up, only to find the blacksmith's son gone an hour later.

"The Castle must have given him a way out," Rolf assured them. "And what's more: half the soldiers are gone. And that includes Sergeant Avery! No one will say where they went, but I'm willing to bet Pogue took them to the pass to look for our parents and Bran."

"But how can we be sure?" Lilah asked. "What if Khelsh and the Council have done something horrible to them?"

"I really doubt it," Rolf told her. "They're too angry about the disappearances. They've questioned me several times, and everyone else from the lowliest kitchen drudge to the other members of the Council. There's quite a to-do down there! Everyone is either terrified or offended."

"Does everyone know, then, what Pogue and the wizards found out?" Celie stopped eating for a moment, looking at her brother with a flutter of hope in her breast.

"They do," Rolf said, taking a deep breath and smiling

at her. "They do, and that's why I think Pogue must have gotten out all right. Even before the Emissary started to interrogate everyone about the missing guards, I heard some whispers. The maids know, and if the maids know, the whole Castle will soon know as well."

Lilah relaxed visibly, and Celie found that her appetite came back in a rush. She tore a roll in half, smashed a piece of ham between the two pieces, and ate it in a few bites. Pogue had gotten free, people knew her parents were alive, everything would be all right.

"Where did you go after we fled the throne room?" Lilah was now eating her own apple in rather unladylike bites.

"The Council sent me to my room and locked me in," Rolf said. Although he tried to sound unconcerned, Celie could see in her brother's eyes that he was angry about this. "Then the Emissary came and demanded to know where I had sent the guards. And Pogue. And when I couldn't tell him, he threatened to keep me locked in my room forever, so I told him I didn't care, since Prince Khelsh was going to kill me as soon as he was named crown prince anyway. That made him leave in a hurry." Rolf smiled without much humor.

"Now you know that Khelsh put his cousin on the Council, too," Celie reminded him. "So you can bring that up, and startle him again."

"Good point, Cel," Rolf said.

Lilah's brow was furrowed. "How did you get out of your room? Did he leave your door unlocked after all?"

"Of course not," Rolf reported grimly. "I went to sleep for a little while, then when I got up I was hungry, and lo and behold there was a door in my room leading to the kitchens! And the door that used to lead to my private study now leads here."

"What do we do now?" Lilah had finished her apple and was wiping her fingers on a napkin.

"You girls should stay up here, it's the safest place," Rolf said. "But I'm going back to my room."

"I'll keep spying for you," Celie said. "I wonder if I could get the Castle to bring us an invisibility cloak?"

"I think you're better off just not being heard," Lilah said. "An invisibility cloak sounds too dangerous. You know you'd be tempted to spy on Khelsh, and he'd catch you for certain!"

"Either way, I need lots more information about Khelsh," Rolf said. "I want to keep him off balance, and know everything he's planning."

"I'll do my best," Celie said.

"And what am I supposed to do?" Lilah was twisting her napkin around and around her hands. "Sit here studying Vhervhish?"

"Why not?" Rolf cocked his head. "You know, if we had known more about them before Khelsh came, we might have been better prepared for this."

"You also need to keep a lookout for Pogue," Celie said, knowing that Lilah would appreciate that duty. "Perhaps he's almost reached Mummy and Daddy. They might come home any day now."

"All right," Lilah said reluctantly.

"It will be a relief to me to know that you're safe up here," Rolf said with uncharacteristic gentleness. "I won't have to worry every minute that the Emissary has taken you hostage or some such."

"What about me?" Celie put her sticky hands on her hips in indignation. "Aren't you worried about me spying on the Council?"

"Not at all," Rolf said. "The Castle would never let anything bad happen to you. You could jump out one of these windows and the Castle would probably conjure up a hundred feather beds to break your fall."

"Don't test that!" Lilah put a hand on Celie's sleeve, but Celie didn't want to jump out the window. She would much rather be a spy, even without an invisibility cloak. And she knew exactly whom she wanted to spy on next: Prince Lulath of Grath. He, and his small dogs, had been suspiciously quiet for the past week. She had seen him at the coronation, but he had only smiled and waved, and not once approached. Was he involved with Khelsh in some way?

But before she could get to that, Lilah had more questions. "Did anyone see you in the kitchen?"

"No, but I had to hide twice. Vhervhish guards kept coming to get some of the staff, to question them in the throne room. Cook stuffed me into the cold room where she keeps the meat." Rolf made a sick face. "I never want to do that again!"

"How much do the servants know about what's happening?" Lilah persisted.

"They suspect a great deal," Rolf said. "They don't like Khelsh, or his men, I know that for certain. Cook started to say something about 'when' Mother and Father return, but then we heard the soldiers clanking down the stairs, and she pushed me into the cold room.

"When she let me back out, Cook told me that they were all being questioned. And a couple of the kitchen girls whispered that they thought I was too old for a regency as they went by, but they may have just been flirting," Rolf said, blushing.

"Probably both," Lilah said crisply.

Celie had to admire her sister for not teasing Rolf more, considering how much Rolf teased her about Pogue.

"So, it seems that the servants aren't happy about all this mess," Lilah went on. "That's good. If you see Cook again, make sure to tell her that Pogue and the guards are looking for our parents, and that the wizards at the College say they are still alive."

"Yes, General," Rolf said, and saluted her.

"I want to learn more about Lulath," Celie blurted out. "Are his rooms really nice? Is he friends with Prince Khelsh?"

Her older siblings stared at her for a moment.

"Lulath!" Rolf smacked himself in the head. "I'd completely forgotten about him! Good heavens, I wonder which side Grath is on?"

"I'm sure that Lulath is on his own side," Lilah said. "But

it would be nice if he wasn't for Vhervhine, at the very least!"

"You'd better go find out, Cel," Rolf said. "And *I'd* better go back to my room, before the Emissary finds me missing."

"And I'll do a check through the spyglasses," Lilah said.

They all three hugged, then Celie put on her cloak and demonstrated it for an admiring Rolf. She put her hands on the wall of the Tower, and whispered a plea for the Castle to open a way to Lulath's rooms. A minute later, a small door materialized next to her, and Rolf shouted in surprise. The door was only slightly different from the one that led to the Council's room. Celie waved to Lilah and Rolf, and headed through the door and down the narrow steps.

It didn't take as long to get to Lulath's rooms as it did to get to the Council's chamber. Celie was there almost too soon, and nearly smacked her nose on the wall when she came around the last twist of the stairs. Once more there was a slit to look through, this one screened by some sort of drapery.

The Prince of Grath's room was indeed very nice. It was almost as large as Lilah's, with an elegantly carved door leading out to a wide balcony, a large bed on a dais, and an enormous fireplace. Through a door, Celie could see an adjoining room full of racks of clothing: the prince's dressing room. The room had lots of windows, and some very fine tapestries on the walls. Celie was quite impressed, and a little jealous. The Castle certainly must like Lulath a great deal. Did that mean, then, that he wasn't part of the plot against Rolf?

Impossible to tell, for the prince and his servants were not in the room, or the next room. It was quite silent: not even the dogs were there. Celie waited a little while, then turned away. So he had nice rooms, that was one thing. She decided to find Prince Khelsh's room and compare.

"Castle," Celie said, rubbing the wall. "I want to see Prince Khelsh's room, please."

A passageway opened up to her left, and she followed it for a few twists and turns, and then down a flight of stairs and around a few more corners. Celie wasn't sure, but after consulting her atlas she thought that Prince Lulath's room had been fairly close to the throne room. By comparison, Prince Khelsh was far away from any of the Castle's main rooms. Not that it mattered; he seemed to walk about the Castle, getting into everyone's business.

At last she came to his rooms, and laughed when she saw them. She was glad the cloak muffled any sounds she might make, but it didn't matter, because Khelsh wasn't in his room, either.

And really, Celie couldn't blame him. His room was awful. It was about the size of one of the cells in the dungeon. There was only one plain bed, which looked barely large enough to hold someone Khelsh's size, a chair, a rickety washstand, and a crooked desk. Through an open door, Celie could see a smaller room crammed with cots where she assumed Khelsh's attendants slept.

Celie had never seen the Castle treat a guest so coldly before. She wondered if his room had always been this bad, or if it had just happened recently. She thought that Lilah had inspected all the guest rooms last week, and Lilah surely would have mentioned Khelsh's rooms if she'd seen them looking like this!

"Serves you right," Celie said to the hard bed. "The Castle may not be able to spit you out like a bit of gristle, but it can still let you know that you are not wanted here!"

Grinning broadly, she went to tell Lilah and Rolf.

Chapter
16

~~~~~~

Lilah was delighted when Celie told her what she'd seen. She wanted to tell Rolf immediately, but they weren't sure where he was. That made them both fretful, worrying that Rolf was being threatened by Prince Khelsh or the Emissary. Lilah paced the room from end to end, muttering to herself, while Celie ate the last of the food that Rolf had smuggled in to them.

Then Lilah went to one of the spyglasses and looked through it, and gave a little shriek.

"What is it?" Celie leaped up. "Is it Mummy and Daddy? Are they coming?" She hurried to her sister, who was already shaking her head.

"No, but look!" Lilah tilted the spyglass so that Celie could see through it.

Celie put her eye to the brass eyepiece and then gasped. The spyglasses always showed things with such clarity that it was hard to believe they weren't in the same room with you, and this time was no exception. But instead of showing the distant hills, the image it showed was not very far away at all.

It was Rolf. In the throne room.

The spyglass was somehow looking directly through all the layers of stone and slate and who knows what else, to show the interior of the throne room, where Rolf sat on a stool in front of the dais. He looked like a cornered animal, his arms folded defensively across his chest, his face set into a hard expression even though Celie could see from his eyes that he was becoming frightened.

"What's happening?" Celie whispered.

"I don't know," Lilah whispered back. "Let me look."

"Use one of the other spyglasses," Celie said. "I don't think it matters."

"True." Lilah went to another window and said, "I want to see Rolf, too," and then peered through the eyepiece. "Oh, good!"

Celie assumed that her sister meant she could see Rolf, too, because what was happening in the throne room could hardly be described as "good." Rolf was not alone, but surrounded by the Council and Prince Khelsh, all leaning in on him, talking in turn and over one another, as far as Celie could tell. Their faces were red and even more set than Rolf's, and Celie could tell that her brother was not cooperating with whatever they wanted.

"We've got to find out what they're saying!" Lilah

kicked ineffectually at the stone wall, her eye still pressed to the spyglass. "Ouch!" She was only wearing velvet slippers. "Hello, there?" Lilah looked up at the ceiling. "Castle? Could you open a secret passage to the throne room, please?"

There was no response.

Celie stepped away from the spyglass. She wondered how many of her ancestors, or any of the kings and queens who had lived in the Castle before, had asked for favors and gotten them. Had any of them even tried? Histories of the kings had been written, but they were always vague when it came to the Castle itself. No books had been written on it, and no one had tried to map it, except for Celie.

She decided to try something.

The sound-masking cloak was lying over a stool. Celie crossed to it and quickly put it on, leaving the hood down and the ties open, since she didn't need to move silently quite yet.

Lilah turned and saw her put the cloak on. "Cel, what are you doing?" She glanced around, puzzled. "There's no secret passage now."

"But there's the door," Celie said, pointing.

And there it was.

That made four times, at least, that she had needed something and the Castle had provided. She felt a little lightheaded.

"I'll bring us some more food when I'm done," she said, trying to sound confident and failing.

"Oh, darling, no!" Lilah protested. "You can't go down there! What if they catch you?"

"No one will catch me," Celie said, though her voice trembled a little. She clenched her fists, willing herself to relax. "I'll take my atlas, and I'll be fine." She scooped up the collection of maps from the table. She also grabbed a charcoal pencil and put it in the pocket of the cloak. "In fact, I think I'll make some notes, if I see anything I haven't noticed before. It will help us sneak around."

"Let me go—" Lilah began.

"You know that I'm better at this," Celie pointed out. "I'll be back before you know it. And you can watch me through the spyglass," she added.

"All right," Lilah agreed. "But just go to the throne room and come back. We'll worry about food later."

"Fine," Celie said, privately resolving to ignore that. Her stomach was already growling again.

She went down the narrow steps with a great deal of trepidation that she hid as best she could from Lilah, keeping her shoulders square and her pace steady. Once through the door and into the Castle proper, however, it became even harder as she realized that she would have to maintain her air of false casualness all the way to the throne room.

Well, beyond it, actually. What Celie was aiming for

131

was the servants' passageway that ran from the kitchen and the other serving areas to the back of the throne room. She was sure that she could either hear well enough through the keyhole, or even open the door a crack without anyone noticing. The door itself was hidden behind an arras.

The Spyglass Tower had been conveniently close to the throne room, so she passed almost no one on her way, just a pair of maids who bobbed their heads and walked on by as though nothing unusual had ever happened at the Castle, and someone she thought vaguely might be Grathian. He, too, bobbed, but with a broad smile as though he had never been as delighted to see anyone as her. She nodded and speeded up just a little.

Soon enough she was going down a long passage that led to the linen storerooms and the ironing room. She turned left, smiled at a maid carrying a stack of freshly laundered sheets, and then found herself at one of the doors into the throne room passage. She noticed that the ironing room wasn't on her atlas, and made a mental note to add it later. Then she ducked into the passage, following it until it ended at a big, brass-bound door.

Celie pressed her ear to the door, but could hear nothing. Her heart in her throat, she slowly lifted the latch and opened the door just wide enough to slide one hand through and keep it from shutting with a bang if a draft caught it. She couldn't see anything, of course, but now she could hear well enough.

". . . reasonable," someone was saying. Celie thought it was the Emissary, and felt herself stiffen just a little. "This is the only possible option."

"To make a foreign prince my heir?" Rolf sounded tired, as though he had said it over and over. "Why not one of my sisters, or one of our own Sleynth nobles?"

"They just don't have the experience," the Emissary said.

"Prince Khelsh has never ruled a nation, either," Rolf said. "Besides, he barely speaks Sleynth and he hardly knows his way around the Castle, let alone the country."

"It's merely a precaution," Lord Feen said. "Your Majesty is very young; Prince Khelsh will have ample time to learn our language and our ways."

"I'll be getting married in a few years," said Rolf in a tone that squeezed Celie's heart. "I'll have heirs of my own . . . probably before this appallingly lengthy regency is through! This seems entirely unnecessary—"

"Sign paper," Prince Khelsh barked. "Sign now! No more talk!"

"Let me read it first," Rolf said in a small voice.

There was some rustling, and then silence for a time. Celie wished that she could whisper to Rolf, and if he'd been sitting on the throne, she might have been able to. She wanted to tell Rolf that Khelsh's rooms were awful, to reassure him that even the Castle would not stand for Khelsh taking over. As it was, she merely tried to send her brother thoughts of love and strength while he faced the horrible Khelsh and his horrible Council lackeys.

"I want to make some changes," Rolf said.

"No!" Khelsh roared with indignation. "Sign, fool boy!"

"Very well," Rolf said, anger creeping into his voice. "But I want the paper to say that you are only my heir until I marry and beget an heir of my own." There was a crackle of paper. "According to this, even if I had ten children, you would still be my heir, and I refuse to sign under those terms."

"Perhaps Your Majesty needs to go to your room, like the petulant child that you are, until you learn some sense," the Emissary said.

"Perhaps," Rolf said lightly.

There was the sound of footsteps receding, and a few of the Councilors sputtering in rage. The door to the throne room closed with a definite bang, and Celie smiled, imagining Rolf stalking out of the room with his head high.

There was some scuffling as the Councilors dithered and Khelsh erupted into angry Vhervhish. He was soothed by the Emissary in that same language, and then at last they shuffled out and it was quiet. Celie waited a minute more, and then she quietly closed the door and followed the passage all the way to its opposite end, which opened into the kitchen.

Where she nearly ran straight into the back of Prince Lulath of Grath.

She made a small *eep* noise, and tried to retreat into the

passageway before anyone saw her. But one of the maids, who had been listening to whatever Lulath had been saying, looked at her, causing Lulath to turn around and greet her with wide eyes and an even wider smile.

"Why, Princess Cecelia! The very one of whom I seek!"

Chapter 17

Celie could only look at him with wide eyes of her own. Seeing his impeccably coiffed hair and immaculate tunic, she was suddenly aware that she was slightly dusty and still wearing the oddly heavy muffling cloak. Lulath really was quite handsome, and extremely tall. He had one of his small dogs tucked under his arm, looking like a limp fur muff.

Celie took off the cloak and arranged it over one arm. "You were, um, seeking me?"

"Yes, *yes!*"

Lulath looked like he was going to embrace her for a moment, and Celie took a step back. The prince was rather alarming, because much like Khelsh, he said everything very loudly. But in the case of Lulath, it seemed to be more because he was excited, rather than angry.

"What did you need?"

"I needed to speak of the matter of the very great

importance, and to check that you are well!" He looked anxiously at Celie, searching her face as though truly concerned.

"I am fine," Celie said. "What is the matter of . . . of great importance?"

"And your sister, the Princess Delilah, is she also well?"

"Delilah is fine," Celie said.

"And you are . . . safe?" The prince actually lowered his voice to something approaching a whisper. "You have a sleeping place that is the safest?"

"Yes, yes, we do," Celie said. She blinked at him, gratified yet uncertain. Did he really care?

Lulath leaned in closer, and the small dog perked up and sniffed at her. It was the color of a caramel, and had a pink bow holding its long hair out of its eyes. Celie reached out and it licked her fingers.

"She like you," Lulath said in a conspiratorial whisper.

Was this the matter of great importance? That his dogs liked her?

Celie gave the prince a puzzled look, and noticed that Cook was hovering over his shoulder. She grimaced at Celie, and held up her rolling pin as though offering to knock the prince over the head. Celie's eyes widened and she shook her head just slightly.

"It is because you are a good person," the prince said earnestly. "And your sister, and your brother." His whisper dropped lower, and Celie took a small step forward to hear him better. "And I," the prince went on, "I also am a good person, and want to be helping you. This regency, I think they are not good. They are with Khelsh, who is very much not good."

Celie hesitated. Was this a trap? Was he trying to catch her saying something against the Council, so that he could report it to them?

A thought struck her.

"Can I see your rooms?"

Cook dropped her rolling pin. "Princess Cecelia!"

But Lulath was nodding. He looked Celie over again, this time with a level of understanding that she hadn't suspected a man who carried around small dogs to be capable of. He held out his free arm to her, but Celie politely shook her head. She stepped around him and went to Cook, who had picked up her rolling pin and was muttering under her breath.

"Cook, it's all right," Celie said quietly. "Prince Khelsh's rooms are very *small*, and *dark*, and *poorly furnished*." She raised her eyebrows, and waited to see if the older woman understood.

"Oh," Cook said, raising her own eyebrows.

"I understand that Prince Lulath's rooms, on the other hand, are very fine," Celie hinted further.

"Indeed, the girl who cleans there said something to that effect," Cook said.

"I want to see what they're like today," Celie said.

"I could send the girl up—"

"It's all right," Celie said. "I need to see with my own eyes."

She didn't explain further, because she didn't really know what she was looking for. She had seen into Lulath's rooms, but it had been through the haze of a tapestry. Were they as large and opulent as they had seemed? And had the Castle provided the furnishings, or had his servants brought them? She had some questions for the prince, and it didn't help that the kitchen maids were all straining to listen in. What if one of them was a spy for the Council?

"All right," Cook said. "I know that you'll be well protected. The Castle has always loved you best."

She said this last loud enough for Lulath to hear. He bobbed his head and beamed as if agreeing. He held out his arm again, and this time Celie took it.

"I'll have another food basket ready in a few minutes," Cook said, again for Prince Lulath's benefit as much as Celie's.

"Thank you," Celie said, as lightly as though she were going on a picnic, instead of hiding in her own home.

"The cook, she is good woman," Prince Lulath said as they went out of the kitchen and up a long flight of stairs.

"Yes," Celie agreed. "She's like a queen of her own kingdom down there."

Lulath laughed. "A good way to say," he said. "I would wish very much that she would come to Grath. She would cook most excellently for us, too, then! But Castle

Glower, it would be fill with anger! I would not take any one person from the Castle Glower. Not any one." He squeezed her elbow in a meaningful way.

"That's very nice," Celie said. "But . . . do you want to stay here forever?" She could not think of another way to say it. Khelsh didn't seem to want to take anyone away from the Castle, unless getting rid of Rolf counted, but he also didn't seem to want to go back to Vhervhine.

The Grathian prince furrowed his brow and thought for a while as they walked. Celie wasn't sure if he hadn't understood her, or if he didn't know how to speak his answer, or didn't know how to answer her at all. She stayed silent and let him struggle with it as they continued down the long corridor and up another flight of stairs in the guest wing of the Castle.

"I do not know," the prince said, stopping outside a broad door carved with the Glower coat of arms: a stylized Castle with the silhouette of some large-winged creature above the towers. "I do not know what I want. First I want to help you and the other princess and the new king be the safest."

He opened the door to his rooms, and Celie knew at once that Prince Lulath of Grath was sincere. She also knew that the Castle liked him, possibly as much as it liked her family.

Lulath's rooms *were* enormous, with high ceilings and wide balconies, just as she'd seen before. The fireplace was big enough to roast an ox, and in front of it was an elaborate dog bed that held two other small dogs.

The one that the prince was carrying leaped out of his grip and ran to her companions. They began rolling around on the luxurious carpet, yipping at one another.

"My babies," the prince said fondly. "They are such the silly things."

"Er, yes," Celie said, tearing her gaze off the dogs and looking around the room again.

They were in a large sitting room, and she could see through a tall doorway to a bedroom on one side, and on the other side was the dressing room full of clothes. The racks were not anything Celie had ever seen before; neither was the dog bed and some of the chairs in the sitting room. But the bigger, heavier furnishings were Castle-made, she was sure: elaborately carved sideboards, a settle with blue-and-gray cushions she was fairly certain had once been in the nursery, and a wide four-poster bed with the Sleyne coat of arms on it.

"These are very nice rooms," she said. "Did you bring these things yourself?" She put her hand on the back of a spindle-legged chair she had never seen before.

"Some, yes," Lulath said. He pointed to the chair and a rug on the floor. "The ambassador said, maybe the Castle, it will not like you, so I brought some of my comforts."

Celie wondered what the ambassador's room looked like, and why he'd been worried the Castle might not like Lulath.

"And of course I have the many clothes." He laughed in a self-deprecating way, waving a hand at the racks in the dressing room. "And my girls must have their bed."

Hearing this, the small dogs raced across the floor and leaped around their master's feet. Lulath laughed again and sat down on the rug, heedless of crumpling his fine tunic. The dogs clambered onto his lap, fighting for position, and one of them scrambled up the breast of his tunic so that she could lick his chin.

"Ah, my girls!"

Celie couldn't help it: she got down on her knees and held out a hand. The caramel-colored dog immediately came to her, wagging her whole body, and Celie stroked her soft ears. The dog licked frantically at Celie's fingers, and she rubbed the little creature's back with her other hand.

"Very much she likes you!" Lulath cheered. "Dogs, they are very good to know people's hearts. And JouJou is the very clever."

"JouJou?"

The caramel dog yapped with pleasure at Celie saying her name, and sprang onto Celie's lap. She promptly slipped off again, because Celie's black satin mourning gown was very slick, and Celie laughed. The dog rolled onto her back and Celie rubbed her round tummy.

"You see," Lulath said. "The dogs, they like you, and I like you, and the Castle likes me. Now you must tell me what I do for you, and the new king, and the sister. What is it that I do to help?"

"Prince Khelsh is a very . . . He is not . . . a good man," Celie said slowly.

"No. Very bad," Lulath agreed. "So bad, his own father say he cannot come back."

Celie's jaw dropped. "He can't return to Vhervhine? He's been exiled?"

"Yes. The exile." Lulath nodded, his face grim. "I do not think the Vhervhish know he is here. I think Khelsh pay ambassador to pretend that he comes . . . by this royal request, which must have been a false thing."

"Really?" Her eyebrows shot up and she couldn't pull them back down. "Where is he supposed to be?"

"I do not know." Lulath shrugged. "I do not think he would listen to me, if I told him to go. Or I would, I would tell him."

Sitting there on the floor with Prince Lulath, watching him play with his dogs, Celie suddenly realized something. The prince, despite his height and his fine clothes, was not as old as she'd originally thought.

"How old are you?" Then trying not to appear rude, she added, "I'm eleven."

"I am two plus the twenty," the prince said.

Celie had thought he was at least twenty-five, if not thirty. But there were no lines on his smiling, handsome face, and he seemed far less imposing with a small dog burrowing under his chin.

"Please, Princess, can I help?"

Celie realized that he had been offering to help, and

waiting for her to give him an order, this entire time. He was hers to command, she thought with a little thrill, but what should she ask? And how much of their situation should she truly confide? She wished she could consult with Lilah and Rolf, but there was to be a banquet tonight, and Lulath's servants would come to help him dress any minute.

Celie took a deep breath, and made up her mind.

"My parents are alive, and so is my brother Bran," she said in a rush. "Wizards from the College confirmed this, but they don't know where they are—yet. We sent our friend Pogue Parry and some of the Castle guard to search for them. We think they're hiding because they're afraid of being ambushed again. Prince Khelsh paid men to attack them in the pass," she finished.

Lulath's eyes widened, but he nodded as though not truly surprised.

"Prince Khelsh and the Emissary to Foreign Lands have been plotting for years to take over the Castle and Sleyne," Celie went on. "Khelsh wants Rolf to make him his heir. We think he'll kill Rolf as soon as that happens."

The prince nodded again. "Yes," he said simply. "I did think something like this."

"Exactly," Celie said. "It's all very horrible."

"Khelsh came to me, to know where you and the Princess Delilah were," Lulath told her. "He wanted look under my bed, and in my dressing room." He tutted and shook his head. "Very rude. I say I do not know. He start to yell, but then the Castle close my door." Lulath smiled in delight. "But first Toulala made water on Khelsh's boot." He gave the black-and-white dog a rub. "Pretty girl," he said. "Good girl!"

Celie laughed. "Very good girl!"

"So you have a place to sleep, and the cook makes you food," Lulath said.

"Yes."

"What else is there that you need? Something else you must need!"

"Yes," Celie said, an idea striking her suddenly. "You say that Prince Khelsh's father does not know he is here?"

"I think so, Princess."

"Would you write him a letter, and tell him what Khelsh is doing?"

Now it was Lulath's turn to drop his jaw in astonishment.

"Why never did I think of that?"

Celie shrugged.

"I will send it today, with my own man."

"Good idea," Celie said.

She hesitated, rubbing JouJou fiercely while she thought. She did not want to tell Prince Lulath about the Spyglass Tower; it would be safer if no one knew except Pogue, Lilah, and Rolf. But there had to be something else Lulath could do.

"Oh!" She stopped petting the dog, and JouJou nudged her to make her keep going. "Sorry." She rubbed the dog's head. "I know what would help Rolf so much!"

"Anything!" Lulath nodded. "Anything!"

"Rolf needs support."

The prince looked baffled.

"The Council is trying to convince people that Rolf is too young to be a good king. If you were to tell people that you think he is a fine king, that he makes good decisions, and things like that, then it would help us so much!"

"Ah!" Lulath nodded. "So very very! I will as you ask. Should I tell that the old king and queen are much alive?"

"Hmm." Celie had to ponder that for a moment. She didn't want to make it too obvious that Lulath was on their side. It would be safer for all of them. "Maybe if you just say that you feel that the Council called off the search too soon?"

"Yes, very good!" Lulath looked delighted. "It will make the Council seem the very bad, if say they *want* old king to be dead, they *want* new king to fail."

"Exactly!"

They beamed at each other, then Celie gave JouJou one more pat and scrambled to her feet.

"I had better go now," she said. "I need to get the basket from Cook, and then get back to the Sp . . . to our room. Lilah will be worried."

"Yes, yes," Lulath said, getting up much more gracefully.

"Please tell her I will help, and your brother also will I help."

"Of course," Celie said.

"If I find out a new thing, how shall I say to you?"

"Put a handkerchief in your sleeve," Celie said promptly. "One of us will find a way to talk to you. Also . . ." Celie stopped and blushed, remembering how the spyglasses could also peer into the Castle's rooms. "I think I can see into your rooms from our hiding place."

Lulath blinked rapidly, but all he said was, "Wonderful Castle!" He seemed to be quite into the spirit of the adventure, and not at all disturbed that Celie and her siblings might be spying on him.

"Also, if I have the news, I will write to you notes and put them under my girls' bed, with a scarf on top to signal," he decided, pointing to the post of the dog bed. "And if I must speak to you as person to person, I will put the handkerchief here." He tugged at one of his lace-edged cuffs.

"Perfect," Celie said in delight. Impulsively, she stood on her tiptoes and kissed Lulath's cheek. "You are wonderful, too," she told him.

He looked surprised, and smiled at her. It was not his usual grin, which made him look a bit daft, but a small sheepish smile that made him seem even younger than his twenty-two years.

"Will I take you to the kitchens?" he asked.

"No, better stay here. We can't be seen together too much," she said. "I'm fine on my own."

"Until a next time, Princess Cecelia," he said, and bowed to her.

She curtsied. "It's just Celie," she told him.

"Celie. Have the good luck."

Chapter 18

Telling Rolf and Lilah that Lulath was going to help them made the Glower children realize something: they could probably be doing more to help themselves. They had been spying on Khelsh and the Council, but they hadn't done anything to actually oust them from the Castle.

But perhaps . . .

"If I can get down to Lulath's rooms to get his messages, why not Khelsh's rooms?" Celie suggested.

"Celie! Why would you—" Lilah began.

"What did you have in mind?" Rolf asked, interrupting her.

If Lilah had been indignant at the idea, Rolf seemed more intrigued. He looked defeated: hair hanging in his eyes, face drawn and eyes haunted. This was the first time he had perked up since they had started their nightly planning meeting.

"What if I stole his sheets?" she suggested.

Rolf snickered, but Lilah shook her head.

"No, he'd only make trouble for the maids," Lilah pointed out.

"Hmm." Celie thought hard for a while. "What if I did something a little bit sneakier? Like did something to his clothes?"

"What, though?" Rolf tapped his lips in thought. "We could spill ink on his shirts."

Celie nodded. "Not all of them, maybe, so it looks like someone did it on purpose, but just on the sleeves of one or two."

"We could sabotage some of them," Lilah said, getting into the spirit of the thing. "Rip it until the seams are just barely holding together, so that it comes apart when he's out of his room!"

Celie laughed. "The back of his trousers!"

Lilah blushed, but nodded.

"Let's do the Emissary, too," she added. "And Lord Feen."

"Yes, let's see how many of the Council we can get," Rolf agreed.

"All right," Celie said. "But we'll have to wait until morning. They're in their rooms right now, and that's too dangerous."

"We'd better get some sleep, then," Lilah said with a yawn.

They bedded down on the blankets and pillows that the girls had brought up from their rooms. Even Rolf, who could have easily gone back to his comfortable bed, stayed on the floor in the Spyglass Tower, as reluctant as his sisters to be parted from one another.

Once she was certain her siblings were asleep, Celie pulled Rufus out of her pillowcase and tucked him against her chest. He smelled like her old room, and she cried silently for a moment before falling asleep.

The next morning they began their campaign. The Castle opened passages for them, and they ran back and forth gathering armloads of official black robes, tunics, and trousers. Lilah made the most delicate of cuts in the seams of the trousers and robes so that only a few threads were left holding them together. Rolf gleefully dipped sleeves in a pan of ink, and Celie used a small, sharp scissors to cut partway through tunic lacings.

Then they had to run back through the passages and return the clothing to its proper owners, which is when they ran into a little problem.

None of them could remember which clothes went where.

Prince Khelsh's Vhervhish tunics, which fastened up the side of the breast with heavy gold buttons, were easy to sort out, of course. But most of the Councilors wore black even under their robes, and all of them seemed to be tall and thin. Celie thought that Lord Feen's clothes had a certain smell to them, like moldy cheese and cats, but no one else seemed able to detect it.

"I'm not that worried," Rolf said breezily. "It will make

it that much more diabolical if their clothes don't fit, either!"

He took up an armload and simply headed down one of the passages. Celie shrugged and did the same, and Lilah took the rest, grumbling that they had left her the largest pile. When they were done it was time for Rolf to meet with his regents, and he went down with the same tunic he'd had on yesterday and a smirk on his face.

"Don't be so obvious," Lilah warned.

"Oh, come now, Lilah!" Rolf protested. "Why would they suspect that I'm behind all this?" But he did his best to act sober and cowed once more.

"I have to watch," Celie said, going to one of the spyglasses.

Lilah went to another, and they eagerly peered into the throne room.

The Council would have already been dressed for the day, so none of their tunics or trousers were going to split at an inopportune moment. But they had met in their privy chamber, so they hadn't yet put on their formal black robes. Now, as they prepared to speak with—or rather, at—Rolf, they would have to put on their robes so that they looked more impressive.

"I hope this is worth it," Lilah fretted. "We barely got things back to the rooms in time. And we're very lucky we didn't run into any of their personal servants."

"We'll plan better next time, I promise," Celie said soothingly.

"*Next* time?"

Celie just smiled to herself. She had thought of something else they could do to the Council, but didn't want to tell Lilah yet. She knew that Lilah would oppose the idea, but Rolf would love it. She wanted him to be there to help convince their sister.

"Shh, here they come," Celie said.

Like a murder of crows, the Council all filed into the throne room, with Prince Khelsh at their head. Trailing behind, with his two bodyguards, came Rolf. He looked rumpled but positively cheerful, though it made Celie mad to see how disrespectfully the Council treated him, as though he were a scribe coming after them to take notes.

Rolf sat on his chair in front of the dais, and gestured for the Council to sit in the straight-backed chairs Rolf had ordered for them, though they never did. They clearly liked looming over him, and Celie had a sort of guilty satisfaction that Lord Feen, who was older than mud, probably had joint aches and wasn't comfortable standing for very long.

The Councilors talked, Prince Khelsh pounded his fist into his other hand, and Rolf sat in silence. He was supposed to sign the agreement to make Khelsh his heir today, but the paper was nowhere in sight. Celie knew that Rolf had taken it to his room yesterday to look over, and he must have left it there. She giggled as she told Lilah.

Khelsh waved his arms some more, and a servant was sent running, likely to Rolf's rooms to fetch the paper. Still

Rolf just sat there, an expression of boredom on his face that seemed to infuriate Khelsh even more. He raised one hand high, as though calling on the heavens to witness Rolf's stubbornness, and froze.

"What is it?" Celie could barely whisper, pressing her eye so hard to the spyglass that it hurt. "What's happening?"

"His sleeve!" Lilah was giggling. "Can you see? Under the arm!"

Celie peered around, moving her spyglass in a little circle until at last the prince's sleeve came into view. The seam of Khelsh's black robe had split right under the arm. It was hard to spot, because Khelsh wore a dark, plum-colored tunic underneath, but it was there.

The sensation of his robe tearing had frozen Khelsh for a moment. Then he hastily lowered his arm, clamping it tight to his side and looking around to see if anyone else had noticed.

No one had, but the rest of the Council did give Prince Khelsh some very perplexed looks as he stopped speaking midsentence and turned to glare at Rolf. Rolf looked back guilelessly, while Celie silently begged him not to laugh or say anything witty, lest Khelsh realize that Rolf had something to do with it.

"Look at Lord Feen," Lilah cried. "Oh, just look, Celie!"

The elderly lord had at last consented to sit, which was probably a mistake on his part. For when he sank down into the straight-backed chair, his robe pulled tight at the shoulders and the seams promptly parted. Now his robe was sliding down his chest and back, exposing his rusty black tunic and trapping his arms as he squawked and flapped about like a surprised crow.

Celie couldn't stop giggling, and neither could Lilah. As the Emissary leaned over Lord Feen to help him gather up the pieces of his robe, his own robe split under the arms as well. Celie let out a cheer and Lilah snorted in a most unladylike fashion, she was laughing so hard.

In the meantime, Rolf continued to sit on his chair, only now he assumed an expression of great concern. He watched the Council cluck and fuss for a little while longer, manfully hiding his amusement as three more lords fell victim to their prank, until the footman came back with the papers from his room.

Rolf said something that looked as though he was excusing himself from the mess. He stood up and nodded regally around at the discomfited lords, his royal air only ruined by the fact that he appeared to be whistling as he strolled out of the throne room.

"Stop!" Prince Khelsh bellowed—Celie could read the word on his thick lips—but Rolf didn't look back.

"Hurrah!" Celie spun away from the spyglass, laughing. "Rolf did it!"

She had not realized until that moment how nervous she was about Rolf having to sign the succession papers. But she had a deep, hidden terror that once he did, Khelsh would plan to have him killed immediately. She could see that Lilah felt the same way, for her sister was visibly shaking as she turned away from her own spyglass and groped her way to the table and a stool.

"Oh, thank goodness! And they didn't accuse Rolf of playing a prank on them, either," Lilah said, resting her forehead on the table.

"Why would they?" Celie tutted over Lilah's fear. "If anything, we need to warn the maids. Khelsh already knows that the Castle doesn't like him; he's sure to assume that the Castle itself is doing these things." She rubbed her hands together. She had a great many more pranks planned now.

"Celie," Lilah said in a warning voice.

"Li-lah," Celie singsonged back. "Only look how well this has gone! And tomorrow morning they'll find their clothes ink stained, and more seams splitting . . . We can't stop now!"

"Too right," Rolf said, coming into the Tower. "That was the most fun I've had in weeks. The look on Khelsh's face when he raised his arm! Priceless!" He smiled and closed his eyes, savoring the vision all over again.

"And Lord Feen," Celie added eagerly. "When his robes just sort of *slithered* down around him . . . Lilah, you're amazing!"

Lilah looked down, demure. "But we do need to be careful," she said finally.

"Do we?" Rolf ran his fingers through his hair. "Surely they'll assume it's the Castle working against them, don't you think? They won't suspect us unless we get caught in the act. And we'll just take great pains not to get caught,"

Rolf said. "We've got the staff working with us, plus Lulath. I think there's a great deal we can do."

"I already have a plan," Celie said, raising her hand as she would with her tutor.

"Do you?" Rolf's eyes gleamed. "What is it?"

"I don't think you'll like it, Lilah," Celie apologized straightaway. "It involves manure . . . a great deal of manure."

Rolf started to laugh again.

Chapter 19

Manure was duly fetched, and applied to the bottoms of shoes, hidden under beds, and smeared in the corners of wardrobes. Rolf and Celie went to the stables in the dead of night and loaded up as much as they could push in a wheelbarrow. The Castle obligingly turned all the staircases into ramps and put all the Councilors' bedrooms in a long row. Celie did most of the work with her sound-muffling cloak firmly in place, with Rolf helping in the rooms where the wardrobes were located in a separate dressing room. They took careful note of which Councilors still had large suites of rooms, since it possibly indicated that they were not firm supporters of Khelsh and the Emissary.

One of the maids caught them at it, and with a giggle she agreed to help.

"I already short-sheeted all the beds this morning," she told them then, covering her mouth to smother a laugh.

"You did what?" Celie blinked at her, but Rolf started laughing.

"I folded the sheets in half and tucked them in real tight. So that when you put your feet in, you get caught," the maid explained.

"Oh, I'd like to have seen Lord Feen's face," Rolf said, smothering another laugh with his hand.

Celie's eyes widened as she imagined it, and then she giggled as well. She had an idea for the maid, and for any of the other maids who might be willing to help.

"Do you empty the chamber pots?" Celie asked.

"Yes," the maid said. "Some of them. And Bessy and Suze do the rest."

"Would they be willing to help?"

"They might," the maid said slowly. "If you—"

"You have my solemn promise," Rolf told her, "as do all the maids, cooks, footmen, and stable hands, that if you are fired trying to help us sabotage the Council, I will rehire you as soon as I get rid of Khelsh."

"Very well," the maid agreed. "What did you have in mind, Princess Cecelia?"

"What if all the chamber pots just . . . disappeared?" Celie asked, her head cocked to one side and her mouth twitching with a smile.

The other girl's eyes and mouth went round, and then she was covering her own mouth again to muffle her laughter. "We take them all down to the scrub room to be washed," she said when she'd stopped giggling. "It will be quite simple to make the Council's disappear. And that awful foreign prince! I'll take care of it tomorrow morning!" She pursed her lips in thought. "What about that other prince? The one from Grath?"

"Oh, he's all right," Celie was quick to assure her. "In fact, if you need help, you can go to Prince Lulath. He's definitely on our side."

The maid nodded. "I'm glad. He's been very nice. I mean, he's got those dogs and always seems to be ringing for food for them, or extra towels or clean sheets, but I suppose it's more because he's spoiled than because he's bad."

"Just so," Rolf said, his eyes twinkling at this description of Lulath. "Now we'd better all be about our business, before it gets light out."

"Your Majesty," the maid said, curtsying. "Your Highness."

"Good-bye, and good luck," Celie said cheerfully.

Rolf and Celie quickly finished spreading the manure around, leaving the last of it under the table in the Council's chamber. Rolf took the wheelbarrow back to the stables, and Celie went to her bedchamber to see about getting some clean stockings, since she had accidentally taken an odd number when she had packed before. To her irritation, there was a large padlock hanging off of her door now, and she had no doubt that the key was with Prince Khelsh. She slipped along the corridor to check Lilah's room, and found the same thing.

Muttering darkly, she went down the corridor, looking

for the stairs to the Spyglass Tower. Her mind turned over and over what they had already done, and wondered what else they could do to sabotage the Council.

"Celie!"

She turned a corner and there was Prince Lulath. He smiled at her, and snatched one of her hands to squeeze it. She smiled back, and reached out with her free hand to pet the dog he was holding.

"I am this glad that I have found you," he said, lowering his voice. "I wanted to tell: I have written to my father, and written also the letter to Khelsh's father. The very day of our talk."

"Oh, thank you!"

"And I have carried this, to find you."

The prince shrugged the strap of a large leather carryall off his shoulder and set it on the floor between them. Celie looked down at it, and then up at Lulath, eyebrows raised. The prince smiled charmingly.

"I thought that there would be things you have not with you in your . . . place . . ." He trailed off, looking slightly embarrassed.

Celie bent down and looked in the bag. There was a cake of scented soap wrapped in paper, a bundle of clean, pressed handkerchiefs tied with a ribbon, a couple of books, a box of imported Grathian sweets, and a small bit of mirror on a long brass wand.

"What's this?" Celie pulled out the mirror and looked at it.

"It is for . . . for checking in the corners. The corridors. The corners of corridors," Lulath told her. Seeing her continued bafflement, he took it and walked to the end of the corridor, showing her how it could be positioned so that she could see down the other corridor. "It is really a tool for . . . tooth doctors?"

"Dentists?"

"Yes!" He beamed. "But I borrow for you. I thought to help you with your sneaking."

"This is brilliant," Celie told him. She took the wand and peered in the mirror, practicing angling it so that she could see different views of the corridor beyond. "Thank you so much!"

"You are very much welcome!"

"I should probably warn you," Celie said, putting the mirror-wand in the bag and heaving it onto her shoulder. "We just talked to one of the maids. She's going to hide the Council's chamber pots tomorrow, but just in case she forgets and hides yours, too . . ." She made a face.

"Ah, I shall be warned," Lulath said. Then he laughed. "Very clever!"

"Thank you," Celie said, blushing. "Also, we've slit some of the seams of their clothes, and dipped their sleeves in ink. And Rolf and I just got done putting manure on the bottoms of all their shoes."

Lulath clapped his hands together softly, shaking his head and snorting with laughter. "You will have them run soon, I hope," he said.

"That's what we hope as well," she said fervently.

Lulath bowed to her, and Celie just nodded, rather weighed down by the bag. She went around the corner then and found the door to the Spyglass Tower and trudged up the stairs. Rolf had already popped in, Lilah told her, and then left to sleep in his own bed. Celie showed her sister the things that Lulath had given her, and discovered the reason that the bag seemed so *thick*: the bottom was lined with a heavy velvet cloak the same dark peaty color as the leather of the bag.

"Oh, this is beautiful," Lilah said, stroking it. She held it up, and it was just the right length to fit her.

"Pogue will be jealous," Celie said, her eyelids drooping. She swayed a little where she stood, and then shook herself.

"Don't be silly, it's just— Oh, you poor darling!"

Lilah finally noticed how tired Celie was, and led her over to their nest of blankets. She took off Celie's shoes and stockings and helped her get comfortable, spreading the velvet cloak over her.

"You take it for now," she said generously.

"Save some of the sweets for me," Celie mumbled.

"Yes, yes," Lilah said, tucking her in as best she could.

"I hope Pogue finds Mummy and Daddy and Bran soon," Celie mumbled as she fell asleep.

"I hope he does, too," Lilah whispered, and kissed Celie's forehead.

Chapter
20

$\sim\!\!\!\infty\!\!\!\sim$

This is very, very bad," Celie said, but the muffling cloak absorbed all the sound before it even reached her own ears. "Very bad indeed."

It had been a week since what Rolf called the Night of Manure Mayhem. The next day had been a delight, as the members of the Council tottered around with expressions of disgust, looking askance at everyone they spoke to, until they realized that the smell was coming from *them*. The howls for footmen to come and scrape their shoes had positively echoed throughout the Castle, and Rolf had gotten quite a laugh out of covering his nose with a handkerchief and pretending to be too delicate to stay in the same room with the Council and their befouled footwear.

Since then, a number of chamber pots had disappeared, as had replacement chamber pots the maids had luckily "found" in a little-used closet the next day. The seamstresses were kept busy repairing robes that mysteriously tore again at the seams only a few hours later, and the windows of the Councilors' bedchambers had all been left open during a rainstorm, filling the rooms with puddles and spoiling a number of books and papers.

The second chamber pot disappearance and the open windows had been purely the will of the Castle, and the Glower children had thanked it repeatedly for what it had done. It renewed their energy, and let them know that the Castle not only approved of what they were doing, but was constantly ready to help.

The Councilors had also awoken the morning after the Night of Manure Mayhem to find that their rooms were in a row in one corridor, with their privy chamber now at the end. This did not bother them at first, until the realization came that they were now as far away as it was possible to be from both the throne and dining rooms. Also, most of their rooms were significantly smaller than they had been before, and only seemed to have windows when it was raining.

Any worry that Lilah might have had about the Council taking out its anger on Rolf or the staff proved to be unfounded. Khelsh immediately started roaring about the filthy Castle playing tricks. Some of the Councilors, to Celie's satisfaction, looked downright frightened at the prospect of the Castle playing tricks on them, and had been seen speaking together in odd corners, their voices hushed and their eyes darting about.

This was exactly what the Glower children had been

hoping for, and so Celie had come to the little spy closet outside the privy chamber to watch the Council squirm while she thought up new ways to punish them. Instead, she found that Khelsh had decided it was time to put a stop to the sabotage.

To put a stop to the Castle itself.

"Ever since I come this place," Khelsh said, "my wizards try control monster you call Castle Glower."

"What do you mean, Your Highness?" the Emissary asked, looking nervous.

Anyone who had been born and raised in Sleyne, as the Emissary had been, had a great deal of respect for the Castle. A respect that Khelsh was clearly lacking.

"I mean stop grow, or make smaller, or move doors. No more stupid hiding pee pots." Khelsh's heavy face glowed with smugness.

On the table in front of him was a lumpy bundle tied with a silk cord. Khelsh undid the knot and let the fabric fall aside. He gestured with obvious pride at its contents, but the rest of the Council merely looked baffled.

Celie didn't know what it was, either, but she thought she felt the Castle shudder, just slightly. Lord Feen noticed it, too, and looked around uneasily.

"What do you have there, Your Highness?" The old man's voice quavered even more than usual.

"Dust," Khelsh said, running his fingers through it. "Just dust. And some . . . things only wizards know. My wizards." He smiled with fierce pride and held up a bit of something gray that was slightly larger than most of the particles in the cloth. "You know this dust?"

"Is that a bit of the Castle?" The Emissary looked pale, as though he didn't want to hear the answer.

"Da!" Khelsh smiled even more broadly, showing a gold tooth. "Dust of Castle. Hard to get. Now we finish what wizards begin, and we see how our boy prince . . . Oh! Our King Glower!" He sneered. "We see how he can be when his Castle is dead stones!"

Prince Khelsh pulled a small black bottle out of the pocket of his robe. He shook it in the Emissary's pale face. "Please, make free to join chant: *Macree, salong, alavha!*

"*Macree, salong, alavha, macree, salong, alavha,*" he said over and over again.

And as he said the words, with a few of the Council tentatively joining in, he uncorked the little bottle and poured the glutinous contents over the dust on the cloth. It made a nasty-looking mud that he stirred with a small silver wand he took from his pocket until the whole thing was a thick, gluey lump.

"*Macree, salong, alavha, jenet!*"

A mighty groan suddenly seemed to emanate from every stone of the Castle, and every wall shifted a bit before settling back with a screech. At the same moment, a great pain ran through Celie, as though something had struck the top of her head and the blow had jolted the nerves all along her left side. She reeled and fell against the wall.

And it was dead.

Celie didn't know how she knew, but there was the strangest feeling that something, some part of the stones, was just *gone*. The Castle was no longer alive, no longer listening to her, no longer waiting to stretch or change. It was gone, dead.

"No!"

Celie tore up the stairs to the Spyglass Tower, screaming.

Lilah couldn't hear her because of the sound-muffling cloak, so when Celie burst out of the door at the top of the stairs and flung herself at Lilah, her sister let out a scream of her own.

"Celie? What's wrong?" Lilah held her, stroking her back until she calmed down, and helping her out of the cloak so that she could speak.

"They've killed it! They've killed the Castle!"

"What? I don't—" Then Lilah fell silent, and turned her stricken face to look around the tower. "It just . . . Did it feel as though something ran through you?" Lilah put one hand on top of her head, pressing down on her hair in remembered pain.

"Yes," Celie sobbed. "Prince Khelsh had a spell, a spell that killed the Castle!"

"What are we going to do?" Lilah, her arms shaking, pulled Celie even closer. "What are we going to—" She stopped suddenly. "The door!"

Both sisters turned, horrified, to look at the wall where the door normally appeared. It wasn't there. All the doors except the one that led to the peephole into the privy chamber were gone.

They were stuck in the Tower.

Celie's body went limp, and she found that she could hardly lift her head. Her parents were missing, the Castle was dead, and she and Lilah were trapped in a tower. Tears ran down her cheeks and dripped off her jaw.

"Celie? Celie?" Lilah laid her down gently on their nest of blankets and shook her shoulders. "Celie!"

"We're going to die," Celie whispered.

"Celie, don't talk like that," Lilah said, but her voice wasn't very convincing.

"We're trapped here. The Castle is dead," Celie said, her voice still the faintest of whispers.

"What did Khelsh say?" Lilah looked into Celie's eyes intently. "Did he say he was going to kill the Castle? What did he do?"

Celie had to think: she could hardly remember what had happened.

"He said . . . he said they could stop it moving, and changing. That means it's dead, doesn't it? I can feel that it's dead!"

There was a strangeness inside her. It was like being hungry, except the thought of food made her ill. Her parents were gone, but she had never truly believed them to be dead. But now the Castle was dead, its stones nothing more than stones; the sense of warmth, of listening, was no longer there, and the silence of it echoed in her ears and hollowed her out.

"Wake up, Celie!" Lilah shook her again, with more force. "Don't do this to me!"

More tears pattered onto Celie's face, but this time they were Lilah's. The sisters were huddled on their makeshift bed, with Celie draped across Lilah's lap, and Lilah was trying to lift her to a sitting position with shaking hands.

"Don't you feel it, too?" Celie still could not seem to raise her voice above a whisper.

"Of course I feel it," Lilah sobbed. "The Castle . . . isn't here anymore. It's all just stones and slates and *things*." She sniffed and wiped her face on her sleeve. "I'd like to give Khelsh a piece of my mind," she said in a hard voice. "No. I'd like to find the biggest pile of manure in the stableyard and shove him into it."

Celie sat up.

"I don't want to die here," she said to Lilah.

"I'm glad," Lilah said with a little laugh that was more like a sob. "I don't want to die here or anywhere else."

"I want to make Khelsh and the Emissary pay for this," Celie said. "No more ink stains on sleeves, I want them out of the Castle so we can"—she stopped and gave a little sob of her own—"so we can mourn properly."

"All right," Lilah said. "But how? We have a little food, so we won't starve . . . at least not today. But there's no way out."

Celie clambered to her feet, accidentally stepping on one of Lilah's hands as she went.

"Sorry."

Lilah just shook out her hand and then got to her feet as well.

"Do the spyglasses still work?"

Celie put her eye to one while Lilah went to another.

"Well, only like normal spyglasses do," Celie said after a moment, answering her own question.

She looked through each of them just to make certain. They hardly ever used the one that pointed north since there was nothing in that direction but some fields and, beyond that, mountains. But as she moved away from that spyglass, Celie noticed something out of the window.

There was a roof about twelve feet below the tower on the north side. It was fairly flat, and there was a balcony farther along. It didn't look like it would be hard to slide down from the roof to the balcony. The trick would be getting out of the Tower.

"What are you looking at?" Lilah joined her at that window. She looked down and gasped. "Celie, no! It's much too far to jump!"

"I'm not going to jump," Celie said reasonably. "You're going to lower me down."

"Lower you down? With what?"

"With the rope that the Castle put here, when it first made this room!"

Celie had almost forgotten about the things that were in the Spyglass Tower when she first discovered it. The Vhervhish phrase book had been one of them, along with the tin of hard biscuits that had been kicked into a corner and left there. And a rope. A coil of rope that had been put away in the big chest by Lilah in an effort to tidy up, and then promptly forgotten by all of them.

"I think the Castle knew this was going to happen," Celie said, and felt two more fat tears run down her cheeks.

Chapter
21

I don't know if this is a good idea," Lilah dithered.

"Lilah," Celie said patiently, shaking out the rope to see how long it was, "you just said you wanted to find some manure and push Khelsh into it! How can we do that if we're trapped in here?"

Lilah tugged at her gown, straightening it, and then adjusted the lace sleeves. "All right," she said finally. "One of us has to go. I'll—"

"No, it has to be me," Celie interrupted her. "I'm not strong enough to lower you down, but you could lower me," she pointed out.

"But . . ." Lilah studied the rope and the window. "I was going to tie it . . . There's nothing to tie it to," she said in a defeated voice.

Celie just nodded. She'd already seen that. The table wasn't heavy enough, and there was nothing else in the room but the trunk, and that was barely heavier than the table.

"All right," Lilah said, her hands on her hips. "You'll have to go. But be extra careful. Don't confront Khelsh, just find Rolf and see what's going on. And if you have a chance to bring back some food, take it."

"Of course," Celie said. "It might be the last food we get in a while," she agreed as she looped one end of the rope under her arms and tied it in front of her chest.

"I know; it's much too dangerous for you to do this every day," Lilah said, coming forward to help her tie a more secure knot.

"And I'm going to dismiss the staff," Celie told her.

Lilah gasped. "All of them? Why?"

"All of them," Celie said firmly. "Every maid, stable hand, and footman; I want them all to quit and walk out. We'll see what Khelsh does with no servants to order around."

Lilah's eyes shone. "Brilliant," she breathed.

Celie tugged at the knot. "All right, let's try this."

Gathering up a few things, like her atlas and Prince Lulath's mirror on its wand, Celie wished she had some boys' clothes to wear, but it couldn't be helped. At the last minute, she put some of the hard biscuits in her sash, in case she couldn't find anything better to eat. Then she hiked up her skirts and sat on the windowsill. The roof looked a long way down, and the rounded red tiles were probably very treacherous to walk on, but they had no choice. There was no ladder, the only stairs led to a dead end, and she couldn't possibly lower Lilah down.

"Um, can you turn, and um, hang by your hands?" Lilah took hold of her shoulders and tried to help her move around. They were fortunate that the windowsill was quite wide. "If you slip, I don't think I can hang on."

Celie got herself up on one hip, her body completely twisted and her palms sweating. "Wait! Loop the rope around the leg of the table, and use it to sort of . . . winch me."

"Winch you?"

"Like a mountain climber," Celie said, trying to remember the book she'd read about mountain climbing once. She'd begun it because it had been Bran's favorite book when he was ten, but Celie had found it to be quite boring. She remembered something about winding the ropes around spikes, though, so that the climber's weight was supported by something other than his companion. "Twist a loop around one leg," she said again. "So that it doesn't pull your arms out of your sockets when I go down."

"I'll try it," Lilah said doubtfully. She hurried and wrapped the rope around the nearest leg of the table, her brow creased in concern. She wound the rest of the rope around her fists, holding it tight, and braced her feet. "Slowly, please," she said to Celie.

"All right," Celie grunted.

She turned herself around so that her stomach pressed against the sill. Her skirts were hopelessly tangled around her legs, and she hoped that no one looked out a window in their direction. Wriggling her legs, she edged out until she was clinging with her arms. Then she let herself slide a bit more, until just her hands were clamped on the edge of the sill, her entire body hanging down the side of the Tower. She let out a faint scream.

"Are you dead?" Lilah's voice was nearly a scream as well.

"No," Celie panted. "I'm going to let go on the count of three."

"All right."

"One. Two." She let out another scream. "Three!"

It actually took her a minute more to let go. Her fingers were frozen in terror and wouldn't release the stone windowsill. But the rope yanked taut as Lilah struggled with it, shrieking inarticulately all the while, and Celie decided it was better to let go than hang there all day. And so she did. Sweat broke out all over her body, and the pain as the rope caught her under her arms made her whimper. The rough stone of the Castle wall scratched her cheek, and she tried to cling to it with her fingers and toes as Lilah lowered her down in jerky inches.

When her feet touched the tiles of the roof below, Celie let out a cheer. Lilah ran to the window and looked down, letting the slack rope slither down on Celie's head.

"Ow! Careful!"

"Whoops!" Lilah grabbed the rope and pulled it back toward her. "Are you all right? Are you hurt?"

"No, I'm all right," Celie said.

But her knees buckled and she sank down on the roof. She slid a little as she did so, and had to jam her feet into the tarnished copper rain gutter to stop herself from sliding right off. Above her, she heard Lilah say something she must have learned from one of the stable boys, or Pogue, but she was too busy getting her breath under control to care much.

"Are you all right now?"

"Yes," Celie croaked.

"I think I'm going to be sick," Lilah announced.

"Don't," Celie said. She untied the rope from her chest. "I'm fine. Tie the rope to the table leg, and I'll yank on it when I'm ready to come back up."

"Be careful," Lilah said for the hundredth time.

"I'll tell everyone where you are," Celie said. "Just in case something happens to me. The servants can get you out."

"You'll be fine," Lilah said, putting on a brave face. "Good luck!" She waved awkwardly.

Celie waved back, and then got to her feet. She did it slowly, with one hand on the stones of the Tower wall, praying silently the whole time. But she didn't slip, and the tiles didn't go slithering off the roof the way her mind kept trying to tell her they were going to, either. Turning slowly, and walking with the hunched posture of a very old woman, she made her way along the roof to the bit that hung over the balcony.

She was concentrating hard on putting her feet just so

177

on the tiles, and when Lilah called out to her, she startled and nearly fell.

"Oh!" Lilah let out another shout. "The balcony is right under you," she called.

"Thanks," Celie called back without turning her head.

Lowering herself to a crouch with extreme care, she crawled to the edge of the roof and gripped the rain gutter. Looking past it, she could see the flagstones of the balcony. She scooted on her bottom until her feet were hanging down, then she pushed off with her hands. The back of her skirt caught on the rain gutter and ripped with a *whooshing* noise. She stumbled and fell, bruising her kneecaps and scraping the skin on her palms as she landed.

"Ouch! Blasted, stinking—"

"Your Highness?"

Celie jerked upright, frightened, as the tall door that opened onto the balcony swung toward her. There was a maid in a long white apron with an equally white face standing there.

"Oh." Celie sat back on her heels, pushing her torn skirts down over her bruised legs. "Hello."

"Your Highness!" The maid dropped the basket she was carrying and threw herself at Celie, hugging her around the neck and sobbing. "We thought you were dead!"

"No, I'm not," Celie said, gently detaching her. "Not at all. Nor is my sister."

"Oh, saints be praised!" The girl raised her eyes to heaven and muttered a prayer. She was about Lilah's age, and Celie thought she was one of the chambermaids. "None of us had seen you in days, and then when the Castle . . . stopped . . . we just thought the worst!"

"Lilah and I were trapped in a tower," Celie told her. "I managed to get out, but I've got some things I need to do."

"Of course," the maid said, recovering quickly. She got up, straightened her apron, and then helped Celie up. She clucked her tongue when she saw the back of Celie's gown. "It's quite ruined," she said. "Here, why don't you put on my best gown?" She moved through the door and picked up the basket she had been carrying, offering it to Celie.

"Why are you carrying around your best gown?" Celie took the basket and looked inside. "Why are you carrying all your things?" She looked up at the maid.

The older girl's cheeks colored, but she looked back with a defiant expression. "I'm going home to my mother," she said. "I won't stay here with that horrible foreigner in charge, not when the Castle's gone all funny and still. I gave my notice to Ma'am Housekeeper, and so did three other girls."

"Good," Celie said, startling the maid. "That's what I was coming to tell everyone. I want every member of the staff out of the Castle by night. You should all leave. Ma'am Housekeeper, too."

"We should?"

"Yes. We'll see how Prince Khelsh likes it when there is no one to cook him supper or light the fire in his room."

The maid grinned with delight, and then helped Celie

out of her torn gown and into the other one. It was plain, but a pleasing color of blue, and only a bit too long.

"I'll just be off, then," the maid said, her voice uncertain. "Do you know how I can get out?"

"I think so." Celie pulled her atlas out of the bodice of her shift. "I've been mapping the Castle for some time now."

"Coo-ee, you're a clever one," the maid said, her eyes round. Then she remembered herself and bobbed a curtsy. "Your Highness."

"I think if you go left at the next passageway," Celie said, hiding her pleasure at the compliment, "you can go straight down the main stairs to the stable. If you pass any other servants, be sure to tell them they can leave."

"Yes, Princess Cecelia," the maid said, curtsying again. She scurried off.

At the next passageway, Celie turned in the opposite direction she had sent the maid, and then followed her atlas toward the kitchens. She went down several staircases and through a large room she thought might have been a portrait gallery at one time, but now it only held some rusty armor piled in one corner. Two right turns and a spiral staircase brought her to the kitchens.

Heaving a great sigh, imagining the warm smell of bread and the welcome she would receive from Cook, Celie pushed open the door.

And found total chaos.

The maids were crying. The knife boy was shouting something, and there was even a dog in one corner howling along. Something was burning, and there was a great pile of potato peels in the middle of the floor. Celie stood on tiptoe to look for Cook, whom she finally spotted sitting in the far corner with her apron over her head, rocking back and forth.

Hauling up her skirts, Celie stepped onto a stool and then one of the long wooden tables. She shouted for quiet, but no one heard her, so she picked up a large copper pot and a wooden spoon and began banging them.

"Be quiet!"

A hush fell over the kitchen at last, broken only by the occasional sniffle. Even the dog stopped abruptly to gape at her.

"Princess Cecelia!"

Cook rushed across the kitchen and yanked Celie down off the table to hug her tightly. Her face pressed into the woman's formidable bosom, Celie patted Cook on the hip, the only thing she could reach.

"He didn't kill you!" Cook's stoic voice broke on the words.

"No," Celie said, not needing to ask who "he" was. "Lilah and I are very well. Rolf, too, I hope."

"Is your hiding place still safe?"

"Yes," Celie said, which was mostly true.

Cook pushed Celie away and dusted her hands. "You're starving. Food for you. And your sister." Cook noticed the chaos of her realm for the first time, and her face purpled. "Clean up this mess! Stop moaning!"

The kitchen maids scrambled to do her bidding, and Celie tugged on Cook's sleeve. "Pardon me, Cook? I don't want— All right, I do want food. But something else, too."

"Anything," Cook said absently. She was briskly slicing thick pieces of bread.

"I want you to leave the Castle. All of you."

The long knife paused, and the maid who was scooping up potato peelings from the floor nearby froze.

Cook turned slowly to look at Celie.

"You all need to leave," Celie repeated. "Every person loyal to Castle Glower should get out." She smiled at the big woman. "Khelsh won't have many people to lord over if the Castle is empty of everyone but the Council."

"What about you and your sister?" Cook's voice was sharp.

"We'll still be here," Celie said, quailing a little. "We have to find a way to stop Khelsh."

"How?"

"We'll find a way," Celie said with a grim confidence that she didn't really feel.

She could see that Cook wasn't convinced, so she tried another tactic. "It will be easier if we're not worried that he's going to punish you in order to get to us."

"My girls can go," Cook said grudgingly. "But I was born in the Castle." She held up the long serrated bread knife, and Celie gulped.

"I know—that's why I need your help," Celie told her,

suddenly finding inspiration in the candlelight gleaming off the blade.

Cook cocked one eyebrow, her enormous arms folded over her bosom, the knife pointing upward.

"I want you to gather every loyal soldier and every farmer and shepherd who can wield a pitchfork or shoot an arrow," Celie said, feeling her shoulders straighten and her face brighten as she warmed to her new idea. "I want messages sent to all of Sleyne, and all our allies outside of Sleyne. Grath. Keltin. All of them. You're all needed to lay siege to the Castle."

Shaking her head, Cook went back to slicing the bread. "The Castle cannot be seized," she said.

"Not when the Castle was alive," Celie said, trying not to choke on the words.

Putting down the knife, Cook turned to look at Celie again. She put her big hands on each side of Celie's face, and her blue eyes bored into Celie's.

"Nothing can defeat Castle Glower," she said.

"Yes, ma'am," Celie said.

She released Celie and looked around. The kitchen staff were all standing, watching. She nodded briskly to them.

"You heard the princess! Gather your things, put the food in baskets. We leave nothing for those rats above to eat!"

The staff cheered, and sprang into action. They filled hamper after hamper, and layered their clothes and personal things around huge cheeses, hams, and loaves of bread.

Cook filled an enormous hamper for Celie, and slid it under a table for the princess to carry away later. She put her best knives in a basket, covered them with clean aprons, and rested a pie on top.

"Douse the fires!" she roared to the staff.

"You'll need to take a secret way out," Celie said, realizing that several dozen people carrying large baskets of food could not simply walk out the front gates. She pulled out her atlas and consulted it. After a moment, she took a page and handed it to Cook. "Lead them this way," she said, tracing the route with one finger. "It goes through the seamstresses' quarters—make sure you tell them to leave with you—and then there's a hidden passage here into the storerooms. You can get out behind the stables, and take one of the side gates."

"You are a wonder," Cook said, tucking the map into her apron pocket.

Celie blushed and stood on tiptoe to kiss Cook's cheek. "I promise we'll have a grand celebration when Khelsh is routed."

"A whole custard tart just for you," Cook said, knowing that it was Celie's favorite.

"I'll remember that," Celie said, feeling cheerful for the first time since she had felt the Castle go dead.

Chapter 22

Celie carefully wended her way through the Castle, catching hold of maids and footmen and guardsmen and ordering them to leave. She led an entire string of footmen through a secret passage and out into the stables, then went back and convinced some of the household guard to go the same way. She was starting to get worried, though, when she realized that she had not seen the least sign of Rolf or the Council.

Steeling herself, she made her way to the throne room. She stayed around the corner from the main hall and used the little mirror on its brass wand that Prince Lulath had given her to investigate. She could see Khelsh's guards standing outside the throne room. Her throat went dry, and she knew that the Council was behind those doors, along with Rolf, or the guards would not have been there.

Celie went back down the passageway to the servants' door. She opened it carefully, making sure that the arras on the other side was still in place, and then put her ear to the crack and listened hard. To her surprise, the first voice she heard was Prince Lulath's.

"This is outrage of the very most terrible!" The Grathian prince's voice was shaking. "You have made hostage the Glower children and done the murder, yes, *murder* for Castle Glower! I cannot sit while you do this horrible of horrible crimes, Khelsh!"

"I lead regency Council, and am heir to—"

"You are the heir to nothing," Rolf cut in, his voice icy. "I have not signed the succession agreement, *nor will I ever.* Should I die, Castle Glower and the rule of Sleyne will pass to my sister Cecelia. The Bishop of Sleyne witnessed the writ of succession this morning, and the document is in his keeping."

Prickles ran down Celie's back. *She* was Rolf's heir?

"Princess Celia?" Khelsh laughed. "Princess Celia where? And Princess Dellah? None has seen them!" Another nasty laugh. "You are alone. Your Grath friend cannot save you. The Castle is mine! Sleyne is mine!"

Celie held her breath, waiting to hear Rolf's reply, or Lulath's, but instead she heard a funny snuffling noise. Then the tapestry in front of her moved, and there was the sound of excited barking. She looked down and saw JouJou, Lulath's caramel-colored dog, burrowing under the heavy cloth to get to her.

"What's this? It looks like your dog has found a rat, Your Highness," came the Emissary's amused voice.

The tapestry was whipped back, and Celie stood blinking in the doorway, with JouJou dancing around her feet in oblivious delight. Celie glared at the Emissary, and reached down to pick up the little dog without taking her eyes off the tall man.

"Celie! Are you all right?" Rolf leaped off his stool and came toward her with outstretched hands.

"Yes!" She tried to run to him, but the Emissary clamped his hands on her shoulders and held her back.

"How wonderful," he purred. "I've been longing to speak to you for days, Princess Cecelia."

"And I've been longing to kick you in the shins for days," Celie retorted, and heard Prince Lulath give a short laugh. "But I had to settle for putting manure on your shoes."

Khelsh roared and lunged for her. Celie dropped JouJou, who landed on her feet like a cat and began to yap, while Celie twisted free of the Emissary and ran for the doors.

"Rolf! Lulath!" she called over her shoulder.

She burst through the doors, knocking both guards down, and ran as fast as she could across the main hall. She went through an archway, then immediately turned right and went into the first room she came upon. Rolf and Lulath followed her, panting, but she didn't stop even when Lulath closed and locked the door behind them.

"I'm sure Khelsh saw us come in here," Rolf whispered.

"Probably," Celie replied.

She was already on the far side of the room, opening the shutters. The window looked out over the courtyard.

She waved a hand to Lulath, who was fussing over JouJou, and felt a pang of guilt at dropping the dog.

"I'm sorry if I hurt her, but you've got to get out of here," Celie said. "Please hurry!"

"She is fine," Lulath said. He crossed the room in a few long strides. "You first, little Celie, and I hand you dog."

"I'm not going," Celie said.

Rolf expelled his breath in a puff. "I knew you were going to say that! We don't have time, Cel, you and Lulath get out of here and—"

"Lilah is trapped in the Spyglass Tower," Celie interrupted. "I have to go back for her."

From the corridor, they could hear the voices of pursuit. The young men exchanged uneasy looks.

"I've sent all the staff away," Celie said. "I told them to summon anyone who can fight to lay siege to the Castle. But Rolf, you and Lulath need to rally the army. We need Grath and even Vhervhine, if the king will stand against his own son. No one is going to follow me into a battle, but they will follow both of you."

Again Rolf and Lulath looked at each other.

"It's my Castle," Celie said. "I plan on being the last one out."

"How will you get out of *here*?" Rolf's face was strained and he gestured wildly around the room. They could hear someone just outside the door.

"There's a trapdoor under that sofa," Celie said, pointing. "It drops into the seamstresses' rooms."

"All right," Rolf said. "See that you use it, then." He dropped a swift kiss on her cheek, took JouJou from Lulath, and scrambled out the window.

"We will win," Lulath said, holding up a fist in a victorious gesture. He also kissed her cheek, then followed Rolf.

"Go through the stables," she called after them in a low voice.

The latch rattled violently, but the lock held. Celie skittered under the sofa, lifted the trapdoor as far as she could, and slid through it backward. She dropped down onto a table in the seamstresses' main sewing room, the bang of the trapdoor hidden in the crash as one of Khelsh's men broke down the door.

The seamstresses' rooms were dark. Celie clambered off the table and fumbled her way over to the door. Out in the corridor, she took the nearest oil lamp from its niche and carried it with her, not knowing whether the lamps farther along would still be lit.

She made her way to the kitchens, and then had to balance the lamp carefully on top of the food hamper, which had to be lifted with both hands. Some of the oil spilled out onto the lid of the hamper, and she hoped that the flame wouldn't find it and set the entire thing alight. Her heart beat harder than it had so far, as she made her unwieldy way through the passages toward the Spyglass Tower.

If she ran into Khelsh or the Council or any of their men, she didn't know what she would do. She supposed she could throw her burden toward them, splattering flame and lamp oil, but the very thought of such a thing terrified her. And if the oil splattered on her . . . she decided it best not to contemplate.

Instead she kept to the narrowest and least-used passages, taking a very roundabout way toward the Tower. And it was good that she did, for when she took a shortcut through the laundries, she found a huddle of laundresses hiding among the great copper boilers, all holding hands and praying aloud for help.

"I can help you," Celie said, putting down her hamper on a folding table.

There was a general gasp and several cries of thanks to heaven.

"Your Highness!" The chief laundress recognized Celie and curtsied deeply, nudging the young girl next to her until all the laundresses hurried to rise and do the same.

"Hello . . . ma'am." Celie couldn't remember the woman's name, and a wave of exhaustion crashed over her. "Rolf—King Glower—has dismissed all the staff. We want everyone loyal to Sleyne and our family to leave at once. Our loyal soldiers, led by Rolf—King Glower—are going to lay siege to the Castle and flush Khelsh and the Council out."

"Then Prince Khelsh is behind all this?" The chief laundress gestured to the room around them, but Celie took it to mean the deadness of the Castle.

"Of course."

"I never liked him," the chief laundress announced.

"That's good," was all Celie could think to say. "If you'll follow me, I'll show you the way out of the Castle."

"A little slip of a thing like you, Princess Cecelia?" The chief laundress shook her head. "I wouldn't dream of it! We'll make our own way and—"

But now Celie was shaking her head. "I'm sorry, but it's too dangerous. If you get caught trying to leave . . . I honestly don't know. I'll lead you to one of the secret exits."

Her heart quailed at the thought, but she tried not to show it. If they were caught . . . she really didn't know what sort of punishment Khelsh would find for them. Still, there really was nothing else to be done.

While the laundresses gathered their things, Celie took her hamper, the mirror-wand, and the lamp and went to the front of the hushed group of women. They crept slowly out of the laundries with Celie using the mirror to check around every corner.

It seemed like hours before they finally staggered out of a small door near the midden and stood there blinking in the waning sunlight. It was long past suppertime, and Celie wondered how frantic Lilah was by now, and if Rolf had managed to round up many soldiers.

"If you hurry straight across to the stables, you can go out the back way, through the pastures," Celie told the chief laundress.

"Thank you, Your Highness." The woman gave her another low curtsy.

"There they are!"

The laundresses all screamed as a Vhervhish soldier came around the corner of the Castle wall and saw them.

"Run!" Celie shouted.

She didn't stop to think of the consequences, she just threw her lamp at the soldier, splattering oil all over the stones of the courtyard. This close to the stables, the stones were littered with bits of straw. The straw caught fire and the laundresses screamed again.

"GO!"

Celie snatched up her hamper and ran back into the Castle as quickly as she could. She hated to leave the laundresses, but she had Lilah to think of. Out of the corner of her eye she saw the panicked soldier running to get something to douse the fire, and hoped it would buy her enough time to get clear. She barred the little door behind her, and then hurried along the darkened passageway as fast as she could, the unnatural darkness and stillness of the Castle pressing in on her from all sides.

It was slow going indeed. Once she got into the more familiar areas of the Castle, Celie moved with great care, and consequently, great slowness. She crept along each passageway, setting down her hamper well away from the turnings and cross-passages, and then stole forward to look with the mirror-wand. If the way was clear, she would hurry back, snatch up the hamper, and continue on, more slowly still, because the hamper seemed to be growing heavier each time she lifted it.

She was almost to the room where she could climb

from balcony to roof to tower, when she suddenly didn't need to look with the mirror to know that someone was coming. She could clearly hear the voices of the two soldiers marching down the next passage. They were speaking Vhervhish, so she knew that they weren't Castle guards who had gotten lost.

Celie looked around, frantic, but there were no doors nearby where she could hide, and only a long staircase behind her, one that she knew she wouldn't be able to descend in time, with or without the hamper.

While she was frozen in indecision, the men came around the corner. Celie stood her ground as they shouted in excitement and rushed toward her. She suddenly felt quite calm, as though the stones of the Castle were giving her strength just as they always had before.

The first man to reach her got jabbed firmly in the back of his hand with the pointy end of the mirror-wand. While he screamed and clutched at his wounded hand, Celie grabbed his elbow and swung him around her, as though they were dancing. He tripped on the hamper and fell down the stairs.

His fellow came after, with hands outstretched to fend off the wand. She snatched a biscuit from her sash, crumbling it into hard, grainy bits that she threw into his eyes, blinding him with crumbs and bits of coarse sugar sprinkles. Howling, he joined his companion at the bottom of the stairs after Celie stuck out her foot and tripped him.

She stuck the mirror-wand back in her bodice, grabbed

hold of the hamper, and ran the way the soldiers had come: around the corner and down the passage that led to the balcony room.

Out on the balcony, Celie faced another problem. There was no way she could carry the hamper across the roof, even if she could get it up onto the tiles to begin with. Grumbling at the foolishness of not thinking to look for more rope or a ladder, she took out all the food and tied as much of it as she could into bundles with napkins. She hung the bundles all around her waist and shoved a flask of apple cider down the front of her bodice, grateful that the maid's gown had considerably more room in the bodice than her own did.

Thus encumbered, and with her knees shaking from tiredness and everything else she had done that day, she clumsily made her way to the balcony railing, then from that onto the edge of the roof. She lay there for a while, uncomfortable on the sharp-edged tiles and with a wedge of hard cheese digging into her lower back, and looked up at the stars. It was very dark, with only a sliver of a moon.

Celie longed to turn herself into a bird, or a bat, or even a dragon, and fly far away. She wondered if the stars were as cold as they looked, and wondered what it felt like to touch one. She nearly fell asleep, but then a loud gurgle from her stomach reminded her that she was carrying food, and lying on the roof, and that Lilah was probably beside herself from fear.

She rolled over and crawled on her hands and knees

across the roof, banging her head on the Tower wall when she finally reached it.

The rope was hanging down, and she tugged it several times. Nothing happened, so she used it to hoist herself to a standing position and stared up at the little window, only faintly lit by what looked like a single candle.

"Lilah! Lilah!" Celie called for her sister quietly at first, and then louder and louder until at last a dark head blocked out more of the faint light.

"Celie! Oh, darling, are you all right?"

"Yes, but I'm so tired," Celie said, plucking at the rope with fingers that still ached from clutching the hamper. "I don't know how I'm going to get up."

"I've made a sort of pulley system with the table legs," Lilah said. "Tie the rope under your arms again, and I'll pull you up."

Celie tied the best knot that she could, and Lilah began to tug her up the side of the Tower. Celie's face scraped against the rough stones, and her knees banged painfully against a protrusion of rock, so in the end she braced her feet against the wall and tried to walk up while Lilah pulled.

When she reached the window, she lost one of the food bundles climbing in, and the flask tumbled out of her bodice and landed on one of Lilah's feet, making her sister gasp with pain.

"Sorry," Celie mumbled. Then she collapsed onto the floor.

Lilah exclaimed in concern, and Celie moaned in reply. She was barely aware of her sister removing the various bundles from her person, plus the mirror-wand, the broken bits of biscuit, and the atlas. Lilah gently undressed Celie and helped her into a clean shift, washed her face and hands, and then had her lie down on their makeshift bed. She brought her some only slightly crushed tarts and a slice of bread with ham and hard cheese on it.

Celie managed to eat while lying down, then she told Lilah everything that had happened since she'd climbed down out of the Tower. Lilah's white-faced horror as Celie told her about her several near misses with Prince Khelsh and the soldiers made her realize how great the danger truly had been.

"I need to sleep now," she mumbled when she was done. Her eyes closed and she fell into a dreamless sleep before Lilah could reply.

Chapter
23

In the morning, Celie was stiff all over and could hardly
move. When she at last rolled out of her blankets, it was to
find Lilah trying to get dressed with similar stiffness.

"I can't lift my arms over my head," Lilah confessed
with a little half-hysterical giggle. "They're so sore from
pulling you up!"

"I wish I'd found a rope ladder," Celie apologized. "But I
completely forgot."

"It's all right," Lilah said. "I don't know where you would
have found one, anyway. And you were busy helping everyone else."

Celie helped Lilah dress, and then Lilah helped her.
They feasted on apple cider, tarts, and sausages while they
planned what to do.

"Clearly we have to get out of the Castle," Lilah said.
"There's no help for it. Hiding here like rats isn't going to

win any battles, and by now Khelsh and the others will surely know that everyone else has left."

Celie felt the floor plummeting out from beneath her. They couldn't leave the Castle, not when the Castle needed them the most! She looked up at Lilah, her eyes wide and her mouth already forming the protest.

"Don't even give me that look," Lilah said. "I mean it." She held up a hand as though warding off Celie's expression. "Celie, there is nothing more we can do. Yesterday I thought that it would be best for us both to stay here, hiding in the Castle until help arrived. But now I just don't think so. The Castle is dead, and—"

"But what if it isn't?"

"What?"

"What if it isn't dead?" Celie felt her heart expanding with the very idea. "I mean, yes, Khelsh did that horrible spell, but . . . what if there is some way we can undo it?" She remembered the feeling she had had when the guards had come toward her the night before. The feeling like the Castle's strength was surging around her again, just for a moment.

"All right, all right, I understand," Lilah said. "But we can't do any of that from in here! We need to get out, and summon the Wizards' Council, and find Mother and Father and Bran. Stuck in here, Celie, I just don't think there's anything else we can do."

At last Celie nodded. She couldn't bring herself to agree out loud.

"Let's see what's going on outside, anyway," Lilah said.

Brushing crumbs from her hands, she went to the window that faced the front of the Castle. She looked through the spyglass and then let out a gasp. Celie got up and joined her at once.

Looking through the spyglass, Celie gasped as well.

An army had gathered on the plain in front of the Castle. There were tents, and ranks of men and horses, and cooking fires, all evenly spaced. She couldn't pick out individual faces, but she could see that some of the men were in the bright yellow tunics of the royal army, while others wore the simple clothing of farmers, shepherds, and other common folk. There was also a bright blue tent flying the falcon flag of Grath, and a plum-colored tent with the twin trees of Vhervhine. And proudly, above it all, was the flag of Sleyne: green with a golden griffin above a silver tower.

"That was quick," Celie said. "How did they all get here so fast?"

"It must be because of Lulath's letter, the one he sent last week," Lilah guessed. "They must have started out then, to get rid of Khelsh."

"Well done, Lulath," Celie breathed, looking through the spyglass again. The great road was dark with horses and men, all coming toward the Castle as more allies joined the siege. "Oh, well done!"

"Now you see that we've got to get out there," Lilah said, rubbing Celie's back.

"Yes," Celie said more eagerly.

They filled a knapsack with food, the flask (now mostly empty), the beautiful velvet cloak that Lulath had given them, the atlas, and the mirror-wand. Celie shoved Rufus down the front of her bodice, for lack of a better place to put him, and Lilah kindly didn't comment. Lilah put on the knapsack, and used her system of ropes and table legs to lower Celie down to the roof below. Once Celie was down, Lilah drew the rope back up, and tied it even more firmly to the table and then around her own waist, climbing down with much grunting and squeaking.

Watching her sister, whose arms were shaking with soreness, creep her way down the side of the Tower, Celie's whole body instantly slicked with sweat. When Lilah was about halfway down, the table in the Tower slid across the floor with a loud scraping sound, and Lilah dropped toward the roof with a jolt and a scream. Celie rushed forward to try to catch her, but Lilah managed to land on her feet, though it looked quite painful.

For a moment the two sisters just stood there with their arms around each other, panting. Then Lilah untied herself, and they carefully picked their way over the roof tiles to the balcony and let themselves down into the rest of the Castle.

The silence of the Castle was even eerier now. The thick walls and heavy oak doors had never allowed much sound to carry, but there was a quality to the quiet that was unnerving. Not only was the Castle no longer watching and listening, but there truly were no people at all.

"Is the Council gone, too?"

Lilah's whisper startled Celie, who was using the mirror-wand to look around a corner at yet another empty corridor. They were nearly to the kitchens and had not seen a single soldier, nor Councilor, in the hour they had been creeping through the empty Castle.

"Maybe they're all gone," Celie said as she led her sister across the corridor and into the kitchens. "Maybe we're the only ones left."

"Not quite. There's a few of us still hanging around," said a dry voice.

Celie and Lilah stopped in shock. There were two Councilors sitting in the kitchens, eating what looked like bowls of very lumpy porridge. It was Lord Feen, and it seemed that Lord Sefton had been released from the dungeons. He was the one who had spoken, and now he rose and bowed to the sisters.

"Please join us, Your Highnesses," he said, without a hint of threat or sarcasm.

"No, thank you, Lord Sefton," Lilah said stiffly. She grabbed Celie's arm and started to pull her back the way they had come.

"We won't hurt you," Lord Feen said softly. He looked even older than he was, his face so creased and gray that it was painful to behold, and his hands were shaking. "We've already done enough damage."

Pity swelled Celie's heart, seeing how . . . broken Lord Feen looked. Then the pity was replaced by anger: How *dare* he look repentant! No, not when he had just stood there watching as Prince Khelsh admitted to trying to have her parents killed and threatened Rolf. Not when Lord Feen simply watched as Khelsh killed the Castle!

Lilah tried to pull her away again, but Celie shook her off.

"Traitors!" It was the first word that came to Celie's lips. "You horrible traitors! How dare you even speak to us? How dare you sit here inside the Castle and eat our food? You deserve to die!"

"Celie!" Lilah took hold of Celie's waist and tried to drag her away.

Celie fought her off, struggling away from her sister, which moved her closer to the two men. She stood there shaking and looking at them through the mess of her tangled hair.

"Celie, please come away," Lilah whispered.

Celie found it interesting that her normally polite-to-a-fault sister did not apologize to the two lords, or even look at them. She took another step away from Lilah, toward the table. Lord Feen actually drew back a little.

Lord Sefton, however, just laughed. It was a grim laugh, with no amusement in it that Celie could detect.

"Your sister is right to shout at us," Lord Sefton said to Lilah. Then he turned to Celie, and she saw that his handsome face now had lines, and there were gray strands in his dark hair. "In fact, Your Highness, your condemnation is correct in all things: we are traitors, and we should leave the Castle."

"Then why don't you?"

Even Celie was surprised by the coldness in Lilah's voice. She turned to look at her older sister, and saw why Lilah was trying to get her to leave. Lilah's face was red with anger and a host of other emotions, and there were tears streaking her cheeks.

"We can't," Lord Feen said. "Khelsh and the Lord Emissary have all the doors guarded. They are looking for you, but they have said that they will kill anyone else who tries to leave."

"So you're *cowards*," Lilah said with a sniff. "I'm not surprised. Let's go, Celie."

This time Celie went with her sister. She wanted to continue to yell and scream at Lord Feen and Lord Sefton, but she knew it wouldn't do any good. Lord Feen would just sit there cringing and looking so lost and *old*, and Lord Sefton seemed to welcome the punishment. Besides which, she could feel Lilah trembling, and wanted to get her sister out of the Castle. If Khelsh really was watching all the doors, they would need to plan their route carefully.

Of course, there were doors that Khelsh and the Emissary didn't know about. Celie was betting she could find at least two that they had never seen before.

"Wait! Your Highnesses! Where are you going?"

Lord Sefton held out one hand to them.

"We're going to join our brother and his army," Lilah said loftily. "Outside."

"Please stop," Lord Sefton said with real fear. "Aren't you afraid—"

Celie turned again and looked at him, stopping Lord Sefton in midsentence.

"I will never be afraid to walk the corridors of my Castle," Celie said. "Even though Khelsh has murdered it. *While you sat and watched.*"

The sisters turned to leave again, but Sefton called them back once more. "The Castle isn't dead."

Celie and Lilah froze. They looked at each other, but Celie didn't dare to look at Sefton. She didn't want to find out that he was lying, trying to gain her favor or make himself seem less of a coward.

"Nothing could truly kill Castle Glower, not unless you took it apart stone by stone. Maybe not even then," Sefton said to their backs. "He could only put it to sleep."

Lilah turned, but only partway. "I don't believe you," she said. "Come, Celie."

"You should believe him," said Lord Feen. "He has some wizardly training."

Lilah turned all the way around, pulling Celie around with her. "You do?"

"I scrubbed out of the College of Wizardry my final year," Lord Sefton admitted with a self-deprecating grimace. "But I know a thing or two, and I wanted no part of this scheme. I know how dangerous black magic can be."

"How did you get out of the dungeons?" Celie put one hand to her mouth, feeling like a fool for not remembering that she had wanted to go down and speak to him, to find out if he was on their side.

"I let him out," Lord Feen said. "There was no point in keeping him down there. We're all in a giant dungeon of our own making now."

"The Castle is *not* a dungeon," Celie said heatedly.

At the same time Lilah said, "Not dead?"

Then Lord Sefton's words sank in, really sank in, and Celie collapsed onto the nearest stool.

"The Castle isn't dead?" Now it was her turn to ask.

"No, Your Highness," Lord Sefton said gently. "It's not."

"I told you, Lilah," Celie said, with a hiccup that she refused to allow to turn into sobs.

"Do you know about the spell that Khelsh used, Lord Sefton?" Lilah was more direct, while Celie tried to recover herself. "Could another wizard undo it?"

"I think so . . . yes, Your Highness, I believe it could be lifted, if the wizard knew what he was facing," Lord Sefton said.

"Excellent," Lilah said. "Come with us."

"Lilah," Celie said, grabbing her sister's sleeve and forcing her to lean down to hear Celie's whisper. "What if he's lying? What if he's trying to trick us?"

"Then we'll just lose him in the Castle somewhere, and let him starve," Lilah said, not bothering to whisper.

Celie let out a short laugh and got to her feet. So did Lord Feen.

"No," Celie said, and then blushed at how curt it had sounded. No matter what he had done, Lord Feen was the most venerable member of what had once been her father's trusted Council. "I'm sorry, Lord Feen," she said in a gentler tone. "But you can't come with us. We're going to have to crawl through a tunnel—" She stopped, not wanting to reveal too much about her planned escape route, in case Feen or Sefton did betray them.

"Oh," Lilah said, understanding where Celie intended to lead them.

"Yes," Celie said to her sister. "I don't think anyone knows about that one but you, me, and Rolf. It's the safest way."

Lord Feen sat down, nodding his head. "I understand, Your Highness. It's best that the three of you get out, and quickly."

"Thank you," Celie said. "Come if you mean to come," she said to Lord Sefton, and then she checked the passage outside the kitchens before gesturing for Lilah and Sefton to follow her.

They would need to backtrack to get to the tunnel, and she muttered under her breath as she used the mirror-wand to navigate back around corners and down dark corridors where she and Lilah had just been. They would have to pass the base of the Spyglass Tower, and work their way over to the ladies' solarium on the southeast side of the Castle. There was a secret passage there that led to the royal bedchamber, so that the queen could come and go in privacy. And from the royal bedchamber, there was a dank little tunnel under the floor that went straight under the outer wall of the Castle.

Directly into the moat.

But if one could swim, and hold one's breath for a half a minute or so, one could swim under the grate at the end of the tunnel, and then out into the moat. And then to safety.

"You *can* swim, can't you?" Celie asked Lord Sefton as they all crammed into a cupboard to wait for a pair of Vhervhish guards to march by.

"Swim? Yes. Why?" Lord Sefton sounded distinctly nervous.

"You'll see," Celie said, opening the cupboard door a crack to make sure the guards were gone, and then waved the others after her as she hurried down the passage.

They reached the solarium without seeing anyone but that lone pair of guards. Celie moved the arras on the wall aside and pushed on a brick that was slightly darker than its fellows. With a scrape, a section of the wall turned on a central pivot, and Celie squeezed through with Lilah and Lord Sefton following. His lordship barely made it through, and she worried that the tunnel would be too small for him.

Rolf had two theories about some of the secret passages of the Castle: They had either been made for Fair Folk, who were much smaller than mortals, or people were growing larger and larger as the generations progressed. Celie didn't much like to think about that first theory. If the Castle had been meant for magical creatures, what had happened to them? Something terrible? What if they were just gone on holiday? Would they be angry when they returned to find mortals in their Castle? Whatever the case, the oldest parts of the Castle, the secret passages, tunnels, and some of the doorways, were narrower and shorter than normal-sized people were entirely comfortable with.

Celie snaked along the passage with her sister and Lord Sefton, until finally her outstretched hands ran across the wooden door that led into the royal bedchamber. She slid her fingers along the left side until she found the little latch, and then clicked it open. She opened the door only a crack, peering out to make sure they hadn't surprised Khelsh in the act of jumping on her parents' bed or something, and then stumbled out into the room. The dim light in the royal bed-chamber was so much brighter than the secret passage that they all stood and blinked for a while.

Once their eyes had adjusted, they went to the fireplace, and Celie took hold of the unlit torch from the sconce by the mantel and turned it around twice. One of the large stones that made up the hearth dropped down with a grat-ing sound, revealing the dark mouth of the tunnel.

Lord Sefton looked down the tunnel, his face going pale. "It's certainly . . . narrow," he offered.

"And dark," Lilah said grimly. "And there's no way to carry a light. Also, the far end is submerged, because of the moat, so we'll have to swim the last bit."

"I—I see."

"Just go," Celie said. "Somebody go."

Someone, probably Rolf, had put her father's crown back on the pedestal near the fireplace. She could not stop staring at it. What if she took it? It would be one more slap in the face for Khelsh, if—or really *when*—he decided to declare himself king. She and Lilah really should take the crown now, when they had the chance.

"Celie, come on!" Lilah was doing her best to hiss at Celie over her shoulder despite the cramped space. Lord Sefton was ahead of her and hopefully hadn't gotten stuck.

Reluctantly, Celie crawled into the tunnel, kicking back at the rock that hid the entrance so that it slid into place. She instantly fought the urge to scream as the dank walls closed in on her. She was small enough to have plenty of room to maneuver, but she guessed that Lord Sefton's shoulders were brushing the walls on either side.

She started forward, bumping her head into Lilah's bum, which was why Lilah had made Lord Sefton go first. Lilah grunted, and called to Lord Sefton to move, please.

They crawled with interminable slowness, and all the while, Celie could not get the image of the crown sitting there, abandoned, out of her head. The trickle of water could be heard ahead, and even a faint lightening of the gloom, which made Lord Sefton cry out in relief and move faster.

Soon he was moving so quickly that he tumbled head-long into the little stream that fed the moat as their tunnel met the larger one. Celie and Rolf had tried to swim up the stream once, to see where it went, but it soon filled the entire tunnel, and they could not hold their breath long enough to find its end. Lord Sefton squawked and splashed around a bit, before realizing that he could stand, if hunched over, and that the water was only hip deep for him.

Lilah and Celie slithered out of the smaller tunnel and into the water with considerably more grace. They splashed over to the grating, and showed Sefton how the tunnel dropped away, leaving a space between the stone floor and the grating that was about a foot and a half high.

"So we have to try to swim under that?" In the pale, greenish light, his lordship's face was decidedly sick.

"Rolf and I have done it a couple of times," Celie said in an offhand way. She was still thinking about the crown.

"And you as well, Princess Delilah?" Sefton turned anxiously to Lilah, who grimaced.

"I've been down the tunnel before, but never under the grate," Lilah said.

She didn't add that it was because she didn't like getting her hair wet, unless it was being washed, and Celie didn't embarrass her, either. She was too busy making up her mind.

"Just take a deep breath, and use the grate to pull yourself down," Celie instructed.

"I'll go first," Lilah offered. "I just want to get it over with."

"That's good," Celie said. "Then you, Lord Sefton."

"I'll go last," he said weakly.

"You'd better not," Celie said. "I want you to help Lilah get to the army."

"Ce-lie." Lilah dragged out the name. "What are you planning?"

"I have to get the crown," Celie said. "I can't leave it back there. I don't want Khelsh touching it."

"You should have gotten it before we got into the tunnel," Lilah scolded. "It's too late now!"

"It's not too late," Celie argued. "I'm small; I can be there and back in no time. Probably before you've even made it across the moat. Just go. I'll catch up."

"All right," Lilah agreed, and gave her a swift hug.

"You're going to let your little sister go back?" Lord Sefton stared at them.

"If anyone can get the crown and get back out, it's Celie," Lilah said simply. "Come along, my lord."

She sucked in air, then sat down in the water, grabbing the grate and using it to pull herself down and forward. Celie and Lord Sefton watched, holding their breath as well, until Lilah's skirts swirled under the edge of the grate and she began to kick toward the surface on the other side.

"Your turn," Celie said.

She still didn't entirely trust Lord Sefton, and so she watched while he took in several breaths, letting them out in great loud *ha*'s before he took one last breath, ducked into the water, and pulled himself under the grate. He kicked and thrashed so much that he splashed Celie from head to foot, and for a moment she thought he was caught and almost dove down to help him. But he finally passed beneath the grate, and then upward on the other side.

With a sigh of relief, Celie crawled back into the tunnel. She went quickly, feeling very light now that she had no responsibilities to anyone other than herself. All the staff were gone, her brother and sister were out, and the Castle might be brought back to life one day. She eagerly slid open the stone door at the end of the tunnel, and burst into her parents' bedchamber.

Where Prince Khelsh was not, in fact, jumping on the bed.

He was placing the crown on his head, while the Emissary watched.

Chapter 24

"Put that down!"

Celie grabbed the cold torch from the sconce by her head and threw it at Prince Khelsh, who dropped the crown in surprise. It clanged on the stone floor and rolled toward her.

Celie tripped trying to leap out of the tunnel and snatch it, and landed hard at the Emissary's feet. She managed to get the crown anyway, and wriggled across the floor with it clutched to her chest.

The Emissary fell over her, bruising her ribs, but she could only let her breath out in an "oof!" and then she had to move. She scrambled to her feet and out the door of the bedchamber, with Khelsh right behind her. There was a single guard waiting outside, but he was too startled to follow for a moment. Soon enough, though, Celie could hear him pounding after her, and the Emissary, too, making three heavy sets of footsteps she had to escape.

She ran straight into the main hall without thinking, and saw that there was no guard on the front doors. They probably didn't think that anyone would try to walk out the front doors of the Castle, under the eyes of anyone coming or going from the throne room.

Of course, there was also the enormous bar, carved from a two-hundred-year-old oak, that had been lowered into its brackets to keep the doors securely closed.

But Celie knew the Castle better than anyone.

As she passed the bust of King Glower the First, she slapped the back of His Majesty's head with one hand. The bust and the pedestal it stood on rocked forward and then stopped in midfall, revealing a mechanism beneath the edge of the pedestal. The mechanism triggered machinery in the floor that raised the bar across the doors.

Tucking the crown under one arm, Celie hit the right-side door with her shoulder, and it swung open on well-greased hinges, hardly checking her flight as she raced out into the sunlight of the courtyard. There were more Vhervhish soldiers there, and the portcullis was down, the drawbridge up.

If she could make it to the stables, she could take one of the tunnels under the moat . . . or the barracks. She'd gotten so many maids and laundresses out safely, she couldn't believe that she would have any difficulty getting away.

"Seize her!" the Emissary screamed, and the men in the courtyard all drew their weapons.

All at once there were too many armed men between her and the stables, which were next to the barracks. She changed direction and ran for the nearest stairs. They only led to the guard tower, and the walkway along the top of the wall, but it would buy her time. She could hear Khelsh's labored breathing behind her, and knew that the stairs would slow him down.

She took them two at a time, thanking her good fortune that her gown had narrow skirts and was a good inch too short. She tucked the crown into the front of her sash and hiked her skirts up high all the same. When she reached the top of the stairs, a guard was peering out of the nearest tower, so she whipped around and ran along the top of the wall in the direction of the Balcony.

The Balcony was really the flat roof of the Sergeant's Tower, which protruded over the moat, and was large enough that she would be able to move around a bit. When she reached it, she flung herself against one of the tall stone crenellations to catch her breath. Khelsh was coming, but none of the soldiers were near enough to cause a problem yet.

Then she heard a roar of voices, several of them calling her name, coming from outside the Castle. She looked down at the army camped on the other side of the moat. She was directly across from the largest tent, the one bearing the flag of Sleyne. There was a knot of people standing in front of the tent, staring up at her with white faces. She recognized the wet black gown and long, dripping hair of her sister.

She decided that the crown took precedence. "Lilah!" She pulled it out of her sash. "I've got the crown!"

"Celie!"

Celie froze.

"Daddy?" She leaned farther over the stones to see her parents standing there, hands pressed to their mouths in fear. "Mummy!"

"Celie, *jump!*"

That came from Pogue Parry, standing beside a tall figure who could only be her brother Bran, all grown up and wearing blue wizard's robes. Pogue waved his arms to get her attention.

"Jump into the moat! It's deepest right there!" He pointed just past the balcony.

Celie had no time to decide whether or not she should jump, because Khelsh and the Emissary had reached the balcony.

"Give us the crown, girl," the Emissary said. "Give it to us now."

"No!" Celie held it out over the moat. "I'll drop it if you come any closer! But it doesn't matter anyway: you're surrounded by three armies!"

The Emissary opened his mouth to retort, but Khelsh lunged for her. Celie flung the crown as far and as hard as she could. His huge body knocked the breath out of her and sent her crashing against the wall as he tried to snatch the crown from the air. As Celie slid to the ground, she heard a distant splash as the crown hit the water.

"No!" Khelsh pounded his fists on the stones.

"Ha," Celie said. Then she tried to crawl away from him.

He didn't seem to notice, but the Emissary did. "I don't think so," the traitorous Councilor said. He reached down and grabbed Celie's arm, pulling her to her feet. "You've caused far too many problems with your little secret doors and your childish pranks. For once you're going to do something useful."

He dragged her over to the edge of the balcony and wrapped one arm around her, pinning her arms to her sides. He lifted her up so that she was standing on the parapet, and there was a roar from the army below.

Khelsh was no fool: he caught on to his coconspirator's plan at once.

"Leave now, or princess dies," he shouted.

"No!" Celie struggled against the Emissary, but the sight of the moat so far below was making her queasy. "He won't do it!" she shouted.

"Oh, I will," the Emissary said quietly. "Just try me."

"Surrender!" Khelsh spat over the side into the moat. "I kill your Castle, I kill the princess. Surrender to me. I am king!"

"The Castle isn't dead!" Celie could just touch the fingers of her right hand to the top of the nearest crenellation. She gripped it now as best she could with her fingertips.

The stone was so cold. "You're still alive," she whispered to the Castle. "I know it."

There . . . what was that? Was that warmth beneath her hand? Was it just because she was touching the stone, or was the Castle trying to wake up?

She drew a deep breath. "Long live King Glower the Seventy-ninth! Long live Castle Glower!" she shouted as loudly as she could, then she snapped her head back and felt the Emissary's nose crunch from the blow.

"Aaargh!" The Emissary dropped her to clutch at his face, nose streaming blood, and Celie landed hard on her knees on the edge of the wall.

She put her hands out to each side to steady herself. Again she thought she felt a tremor pass through the stone, but it might have just been from the way she was shaking. Then she jumped backward onto safer footing and ran, but Khelsh was ready for her. He caught her just as she reached the side of the Balcony that overlooked the courtyard. He spun her around, and it was then that she saw the knife in his other hand. Celie brought her knee straight up, as hard as she could.

"That's for me, and Lilah, and Ro—" But her triumphant shout ended in a shriek as the prince, despite being doubled over in pain, lashed out with the knife.

They both looked in surprise at the blood that was spreading across her sleeve.

Clutching the wound, Celie spun around and ran down the walkway. The Vhervhish guards were no longer milling about uncertainly: one had come up to block the staircase. There were two more in the tower beyond.

Celie was trapped. She rested her wounded arm on the parapet, and felt the stone grow warm beneath her hand. Her heart gave a little flutter.

"A good fight," Khelsh conceded, though his voice still sounded strained. He did manage to come toward her without limping. "But now is over. No more silliness." With the knife, he beckoned for her to come toward him.

Celie didn't think she could run anymore. Or hide. She had nowhere else to go, and she didn't want to be the reason why her family lost the Castle. Her legs were shaking, and a single drop of blood fell onto the gray stones of the Castle.

She turned and stepped into the nearest crenellation. She swayed a little, and put out both hands to brace herself. Across the moat she saw her family, and her friends. Lulath was there, and Pogue. She even saw Cook, armed with a large cleaver.

"Jump!" Bran waved his arms to get her attention. "Jump into the moat!"

Celie nodded, not sure if he could tell. Her throat was so dry, she didn't think she could shout anymore. She didn't have the strength to jump, either. Inside her bodice, Rufus was making her uncomfortably hot and sweaty. She pulled him out and tucked him under her arm.

"Oh! Your doll, baby?" Khelsh made horrible fake baby crying noises, coming forward a few more paces.

Celie turned away from him, getting ready to jump, and Rufus fell to the ground. She bent down to pick him up, but before she could, the stones under her feet rippled, and Rufus *changed*.

A lion, a winged lion—a griffin, like the one on the flag—stood between her and Khelsh now. Khelsh dropped his knife in terror. Celie stepped backward toward the court-yard stairs as the griffin lunged at Khelsh. She stepped back farther, and suddenly there was nothing beneath her feet. One of Khelsh's guards snatched at her, snagging the skirt of her gown, but he was too late.

Princess Celie plummeted to the courtyard below.

Chapter 25

"I knew the Castle loved you best," Rolf said gently into Celie's ear.

His breath blew hair into her ear, and it tickled. She tried to brush him away, but someone was holding her arms down. She tried to open her eyes and look, but there was a cool, wet cloth over her eyes. She could hear a great many voices, and the clatter of men walking in armor, and other footsteps in heavy boots.

"Just rest, my darling," said her mother.

"We'll need you to stand back, Your Majesty," Pogue said politely.

"Are you sure you've got her?" Her mother's voice was anxious.

"She weighs about as much as a newborn foal," Pogue said.

"As light as the plume of a cap," said Prince Lulath, and then Celie felt herself rising into the air.

Pogue and Lulath carried her from the brightness into a dim coolness that was just as loud with footsteps and voices. A great feeling of warmth and love enveloped Celie, and she knew that they were in the main hall.

And the Castle had come back to life.

"I missed you," she murmured.

"That's why I came back," Pogue said in a teasing voice.

"Are you flirting with *another* of my sisters?" Rolf sounded aggrieved. "Is no woman safe from you?"

"Boys, stop that," the queen said indulgently. "Ah! There's her room, just there."

"I'm surprised the Castle didn't put it right *in* the main hall," Pogue remarked as they turned into a room whose familiar smells greeted Celie like an old friend. "Have you got her, Bran?"

Strong arms lifted her from the litter and placed her on her own bed.

"What happened?" Celie finally had the strength to ask as she snuggled down into the pillows. Her right arm twinged, and strong hands gently took hold of it again.

"Here, put it on this." Bran nested her arm in a pillow.

"The Castle caught you," Rolf said, and the edge of the bed sank down as he sat on it. "No one has ever seen anything like it. The stones seemed to go soft under you, and you were lying there like an empress in a bed of silk when we reached you."

"What about Khelsh?" Celie struggled to sit up, knocking the compress aside with her good hand, but Bran pushed her back down. She smiled up at her brother. His face was thinner than when last she'd seen him, and he had a freshly healed scar above his left eyebrow.

"Khelsh," Rolf began, but their mother hissed at him.

"Carried off by that griffin, wherever it came from," Pogue said. When the queen gave him a look, he shrugged. "She would find out eventually, Your Majesty," he said. "It snatched him up, and then it just . . . disappeared."

"Oh," was all Celie could think to say. So Khelsh was dead, or as good as. She looked up at her mother and Bran again. "Where have you been?" Tears trickled out of her eyes.

The queen sat on the other side of the bed and put her arms around Celie. "I'm so sorry, my darling. Your father and Bran were badly hurt, and I didn't know whom we could trust. Bran managed to use magic to protect us during the ambush, and we made our way to a little shepherd's cottage. That good man and his wife hid us until your father had recovered. Pogue found us just as we had decided to risk coming home. There were assassins still looking for us; we were attacked again on our way here, but fortunately Sergeant Avery's men were able to dispatch them."

"The worst part has been convincing Father not to declare war on Vhervhine," Bran said with a crooked smile. "We ran into King Kharth and his men, and Father was certain that the story of Khelsh being exiled was all a ruse. It took days of talk for us all to get to trusting one another."

"Khelsh would have much loved big war between Sleyne and Vhervhine," Lulath said, shaking his head. "And Grath, too. It has been no harvest festival, this week."

"I don't know about a party," King Glower said, coming into the room. "But what about a celebratory feast?"

"Daddy!" Celie held out her arms to him, and he limped to her bed and embraced her.

"My Celia-delia," he said fondly. "Thank you for protecting the Castle, and your brother and sister, for me."

"Excuse me?" Rolf looked affronted. "I think I did a rather good job at being a king!"

"And I'm not sure if what Celie did was brave or foolish," said Lilah, who had followed their father into the room. "Jumping off the battlements! Calling up a griffin from who-knows-where!" But she couldn't keep the smile off her face.

"You are very bravest of the girls," Lulath said.

"No, I'm tired," Celie said.

Everyone laughed, and Celie blushed, feeling childish, but she couldn't find the strength to do much else. The queen herded everyone out, after they had all stooped to kiss Celie's cheek, including Lulath, and to her further embarrassment, Pogue. Last of all her parents kissed her, and then left her to sleep.

But Celie wasn't alone.

"I really have missed you," she murmured sleepily to the Castle.

The curtains over her windows closed, and Castle Glower painted the ceiling of her room dark like the night sky, twinkling with thousands of gemlike stars.

Acknowledgments

From that sudden lightning flash of "Hey, magic castle!" that strikes late at night to seeing your book on a bookstore or library shelf, a lot of people have to pitch in. My family and friends are always there to cheer me on, and I love them so much for that (and so much more). We are also very lucky to live on the same block as two of the world's best babysitters. Thank you, Miranda and Ethan, for playing Indiana Jones and Slidebaby for endless hours while I wrote. And while the children were thus engaged, I was at my local library, which is happily full of very nice chairs, very nice books, and even nicer librarians!

Thanks are also due to my dear patient agent and friend, Amy Jameson, who doesn't cry with frustration (even though I'm convinced she secretly wants to) when I call her up to tell her about a brand-new book . . . even though I haven't finished the book I'm supposed to be working on.

And thanks, so many thanks, go to Melanie Cecka, who said a resounding "Yes!" to me after so many editors had said "No!" This book is lovingly dedicated to her, for that "Yes!" and for knowing that I had a book like this in me.

Want more magic from Jessica Day George?
Read on for an excerpt from *Dragon Slippers*.

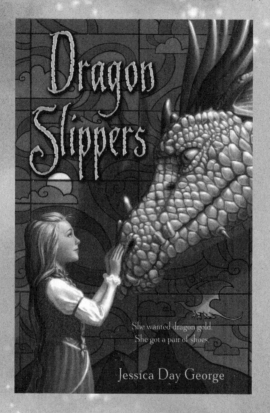

In this charming fantasy, young Creel makes a bargain with a dragon for a seemingly simple pair of blue slippers. But these aren't just ordinary shoes. They could save Creel's kingdom . . . or destroy it.

"A magical, fun-filled page-turner. . . . A far cry from an old-school Cinderella story." —*Bookpage*

A Fine Pair of Shoes

While I sat glumly on a stone outcropping with my pitiful bundle of belongings beside me, the brown dragon dispersed the image of my aunt and her audience and summoned his blue-gray friend again. I was trying to think of some alternative, some way that I could get out of this mess and go home. . . . No, not home. I didn't have a home anymore, and I was old enough to make my own way in the world, one way or another.

First, however, I needed to get out of this cave.

"The Lord of Carlieff's son is coming," Theoradus told his friend in a dry growl, "to rescue the fair maiden."

"*Is* she fair?" His friend squinted up out of the water at me. "I never can tell with these humans." He shook his head. "Is he decked out in shining armor and already madly in love with the poor maiden?"

"Yes," Theoradus admitted, an expression of distinct embarrassment crossing his face.

The other dragon roared with what I realized was laughter. "I might come and watch. Earnest young knights are my favorite sport. I love the looks on their faces when they realize that they're being slow-cooked in their own armor."

An idea was forming in my brain, though I had to take a moment to quell the horrifying image of the lord's son being slow-cooked in his own armor. This outer chamber of the dragon's lair was very plain, but there was a wide opening beyond the pool that surely led to more caves.

I hopped down from my cold seat. "If I may suggest something," I began.

"No," the brown dragon said curtly.

"If you would please listen to me, I could save you the inconvenience of having to fight the lord's son," I wheedled.

"No one asked you," Theoradus retorted.

"But I don't want to stay here and have you fight him," I said, taking a bold step toward the beast. "And you don't want to fight him, either."

"What is it trying to say?" The blue-gray dragon peered curiously up at me. There was a look of amusement on its muzzle.

"I will happily leave here, and take the lord's son with me," I said in a rush. "That way, you won't have to worry about me, or fighting the lord's son or any other knight. And all I ask in return is a small trinket from your large and no doubt magnificent hoard."

A single jewel-encrusted goblet from the dragon's hoard would pay my way to a city . . . perhaps even to the King's Seat itself. . . . And surely the dragon would not miss a single item from what I was sure was a prodigious treasure trove, considering his age.

"You want something from my hoard?" The brown dragon looked stunned.

My heart sank. Perhaps in dragon society this was a horrible faux pas. I prayed fervently that it wasn't the sort of mistake that was remedied by roasting the offender.

The other dragon guffawed, stirring the water of the pool from underneath. "What in the name of the Seven Volcanoes do you want a pair of shoes for?"

"I beg your pardon?" I stared from one dragon to the other. "Shoes? A pair of—No . . . I wanted . . . a goblet or some such."

"A goblet?" The brown dragon looked mystified. "I don't collect dinnerware."

The other snorted, rippling the surface of the pool. "She's heard the stories," he explained. "She thinks we all lounge about on piles of gold."

"You don't?" My voice was a squeak.

"Of course not," Theoradus said. "Well, I'm sure there are some who do. It takes all kinds. I myself fancy shoes." His golden eyes half-closed. "There's just something so fascinating about the way they're made, and the way the styles change over the years. . . ."

The blue-gray dragon in the pool was laughing quietly,

a sound that made my eyes water. "Go on then! Let her take a pair of shoes if she likes, and be off!"

I looked down at my rough sandals. I thought again about going back. I thought about my aunt and the bed I shared with my cousins, who pinched me when they wanted more blankets.

"One pair of shoes," I bargained with the brown dragon of Carlieff, feeling my heart hammering in my chest at my boldness. "And I'll never trouble you again."

There was a long, terrible silence.

"Oh, why not?" He sighed. "Come this way."

He led me past the pool where the image of the other dragon still laughed, and through the entrance to the inner chamber of his lair. Here, too, I was disappointed as this proved to be just another large cavern, but with a huge oval depression in the floor to one side that I suspected might be the dragon's bed. Beyond the bed was yet another rough opening and this one was curtained by a large and somewhat moldy tapestry.

The dragon pulled the tapestry aside with a gesture that was almost reverent, and motioned with his foreclaw for me to precede him into the inner cave. I took a deep breath, still secretly hoping for a pile of gold, and stepped forward.

Shoes. Shoes as far as the eye could see. This third cavern was the largest yet, and every square foot of it was covered in wooden racks holding shoes. Women's shoes, men's shoes, children's shoes. There were boots and dancing slippers and sandals. Shoes made of cloth and leather and wood. There were fanciful pointed slippers with bells on the upturned toes and men's work boots with thick soles.

I marveled at fur-lined boots embroidered with red silk and clusters of small shells. The dragon watched carefully as I caressed a pair of high-heeled dancing slippers so encrusted with emeralds that I doubted the wearer would be able to walk in them, let alone dance. I could not imagine what sort of person would wear such shoes, and I stopped to imagine briefly where the woman had lived, and when.

"Make your choice," the dragon said as I reached out a hand to a tiny pair that were apparently carved of crystal. The dragon's voice sounded nervous, and I wondered if he was afraid that my rough peasant's hands would damage the delicate footwear.

I withdrew my hand and moved on, searching for shoes that looked to be my size. Something sensible, I thought, boots perhaps, or at the least, sturdy brogues.

Nevertheless I paused before a delicate pair of green satin slippers embroidered with gold. My mother would have loved them, I thought with a pang. I remembered how she had sighed over some of the fancy embroidery that she had done for the wealthy women of the town. It had always saddened me that she was forced to wear such plain gowns, when all the while she was toiling over beautiful and intricate garments for women who did not even look her in the eyes when they paid her.

"No, Creel," I told myself firmly, moving on. "You have to be sensible."

Sensible. I was not going back to Carlieff Town. I had to make my own way in the world, and if I was going to take a pair of shoes, they would need to reflect that.

I began looking at sturdy shoes with thick soles. They should fit well and be comfortable, or there was no point in having them at all. Fortunately, in the six hundred or so years that the brown dragon had been collecting shoes, he had amassed quite an array in all shapes and sizes, and I soon had a large selection to try on.

He still seemed tense about me touching his hoard, but I was careful to treat each pair gently, no matter how plain or fancy. I set them down on the far side of the room and crouched down to see which ones fit.

The embroidered slippers made me think of my vague plan, and as I tried on pair after pair of shoes, I worked it over. My mother had taught me to embroider, and to knot and weave sashes and lace. She herself had been an assistant dressmaker in the King's Seat, before a visit to some cousins had resulted in her meeting and marrying my father. She had never let me do anything for an actual customer, explaining that they had paid her to do the work and she had an obligation to do it. She had trained me using scraps of fabric and tag ends of thread, and I could admit without any false modesty that I was good. Very good, in fact. After I surpassed even my mother's skill, she had often lamented that my talent would be wasted in Carlieff, with no money to send me to a larger city where I might find a place at a fancy shop.

I had thought that with a piece of the brown dragon's hoard I could pay my way to a city and buy the materials

I would need for a sampler set to show potential employers. If I was as accomplished as Mother had said, then I hoped to earn enough to one day open my own shop. But without silver to buy what I needed, I would have to try another way. Perhaps if I went to the King's Seat, where I was totally unknown, and claimed that bandits had robbed me of nearly everything during the journey, the scanty bits of cloth and yarn I had with me would be enough to find me a job.

I had been so caught up in my plans that it took me a moment to realize that I had gone through all the shoes I had originally selected and none of them fit. I heaved a sigh and put them all back, then began searching for more. Perhaps some sturdy boots meant for a boy, or a better pair of sandals would have to do.

There was a sound from the outer cavern, and the dragon left off his anxious scrutiny of me. I gathered from the rumbling that his friend was impatient to hear what was happening.

At the far end of the last row of shelves I found a strange pair of shoes. Well, not really all that strange—they were sitting beside two somethings made of black and white feathers, which could not possibly fit human feet—but they caught my attention nonetheless. They were a rich azure blue, and made from very soft, thick leather. They had no laces, but slipped over the foot to reach a little way up the front and back of the ankle. The heels were low, the soles were made of some stiffer dark gold leather, and the interiors were lined with white silk.

They were much too fancy for my needs, but I couldn't tear my eyes from them all the same. They looked to be just my size, and terribly comfortable. Besides, I reasoned, they were obviously new and of good quality. And if I wanted to pass myself off as a master artisan I would need to dress better.

And that meant wearing nice shoes.

I picked them up and went back to the center of the room, where I had been gathering another group of shoes to try on. I left the blue slippers for last, but I already knew in my gut that they would be the only pair that fit.

I was right.

None of the boots or sandals, the brogues or even the crude moccasins I thought came from the southlands fit my feet. They were too big or too small, the toe pinched or the heel did. They were too stiff, or too floppy, for proper walking.

And then I slipped into the blue pair.

They fit as though they had been made for my feet. They were so light that I felt as if I were barefoot, yet the soles were thick enough that I could not feel the uneven stone floor beneath them. They were supple as I walked and didn't slide or chafe my feet. I had a sudden urge to cut the skirt of my gown off at the knee so that everyone could admire my beautiful new shoes.

"By the Seven Volcanoes!" The brown dragon had returned, and steam was rising from his nostrils as he surveyed my footwear. "What are you doing?"

I was taken aback by his reaction. "You said I could

have any pair of shoes that I wanted," I said stubbornly. I had never owned anything as nice as these shoes, and longing for them made me bold. "And these are the only ones that fit me. I want these."

"Any shoes but those!"

I frowned up at him. "No, it was to be any shoes I liked. You never said that there were some pairs I could not have!"

"What's going on?" The voice of the blue-gray came wafting into the shoe cave. "Which shoes did she pick?"

"She picked the—" Theoradus began, roaring back over his winged shoulder to the cave entrance. "She picked the—" Then he looked back at me and snapped his fanged muzzle shut.

"You said any pair of shoes," I reminded him. "Or I will stay here, and let my aunt rouse the entire town to come after you." I folded my arms and put my chin in the air. "You gave your word just as I gave mine."

"You don't know what you're doing," the brown dragon said, its eyes narrowed to slits.

"They're only shoes," I pointed out. "They are very nice," I hastened to add. "And they are certainly the finest slippers I have ever worn. They fit me perfectly."

Theoradus studied me carefully for some minutes, while the sound of the blue-gray's voice grew ever more petulant. The brown monster stared at the shoes, still visible because I was holding up my skirt so that I could admire them, too. He looked into my face, and smoke continued to billow from his nostrils, making my eyes water.

"Just a pair of shoes, you say?" His voice was rougher than normal. "I did indeed give my word. And you will hold me to it?"

Mute and confused, all I could do was nod.

He heaved an enormous sigh, even more bone-rattling than the ones he had emitted when I'd first arrived, and then he turned away.

"Then—I may keep them?" I called after him.

"I gave my word," came the heavy reply. "You wish to have those shoes, and I cannot refuse you." There was the scraping of his claws on stone as he walked back through the sleeping chamber. "She has selected a pair of shoes," I heard him tell the blue-gray dragon.

"Oh, come now!" The other dragon was obviously still highly amused by the situation. "Did she winkle out your favorite pair? You look as though your fire has gone out!"

"Come forward, girl," Theoradus snapped. "And show Amacarin which shoes you have chosen."

Still holding my skirts at my knees, I walked over to the edge of the pool and held first one foot and then the other over the water. The blue-gray dragon reflected there hissed and drew back in shock. His eyes flicked from my feet to Theoradus and back several times before he could speak.

"*Those shoes?*" He was gasping for air. "Out of all the foolish human footgear you have collected over the years, she selected *those*? Why do you even have them?"

The great brown dragon bristled, literally, at having his hoard referred to as "foolish," but he did not otherwise reply. I looked from one beast to the other. "What is so remarkable about these shoes?"

Amacarin, as the blue-gray was apparently named, hissed again. "Those shoes—"

"Those shoes were made by a master craftsman, many years ago," Theoradus interrupted. "And no dragon parts lightly with something he treasures."

"Especially something like—" Amacarin began.

"*Any* choice would have been difficult for me to see on your feet," Theoradus broke in.

"Er," I said. "Well, I'm . . . sorry . . . to have upset you." I looked from one dragon to the other, but neither spoke for a long time.

Then Theoradus turned to me. "You have your shoes, girl, now go. And remember to keep your part of the bargain."

"Yes . . . sir," I squeaked, my attention being drawn from my new shoes to the fact that I was standing just a pace away from a large and upset dragon.

I let go of my skirts and hustled back to the shoe room to fetch my things, slipping my old sandals into the bundle just in case. I had toyed with the idea of leaving them behind, a little addition to the dragon of Carlieff's collection, but decided they were far too crude and shabby. Besides, I might want to wear them for a while, to spare my new shoes.

"Thank you, sir," I said sincerely as I made my way out of the caves. "You have been most kind and understanding about this whole, er, business."

"I have kept my part of the bargain," Theoradus said. "Now you must keep yours."

"Yes, indeed," I replied, and hurried down the path toward Carlieff Town.

JESSICA DAY GEORGE

is the author of several books for Bloomsbury,
including *Princess of the Silver Woods*, as well
as three novels in the Dragon Slippers series.
Originally from Idaho, she studied at Brigham
Young University and has worked as a movie
store clerk, a bookseller, and a school office
lady before becoming a writer. Jessica lives in
Salt Lake City, Utah, with her husband, three
children, and a very small dog. Her favorite
day of the week is Friday because often there is
pizza for dinner.

www.JessicaDayGeorge.com

And you thought Tuesdays were extraordinary?
Just *wait* until Wednesday!

Don't miss Princess Celie and Castle Glower
when they return in . . .

Wednesdays
in the
Tower

by JESSICA DAY GEORGE

In this exciting sequel to *Tuesdays at the Castle*, Princess Celie
discovers a brand-new room in Castle Glower—with a giant
egg inside! The Castle wants Celie to care for what hatches,
but as new threats arise both inside and outside the kingdom,
will she be up for the challenge?

From dragons
to princesses
to mysterious castles . . .

Don't miss the magic of fantasy and fairy tale from

Jessica Day George

www.JessicaDayGeorge.com
www.bloomsburykids.com

Looking for even more Magic in your life?

The Magic Half

ANNIE BARROWS

The New York Times Bestselling Author

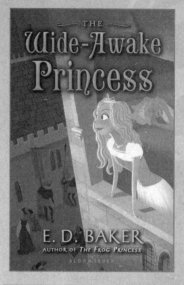

THE Wide-Awake Princess

E. D. BAKER

AUTHOR OF *The Frog Princess*

BLOOMSBURY

Dare to be ordinary

ORDINARY MAGIC

Caitlen Rubino-Bradway

BLOOMSBURY

DRAGONBORN

Toby Forward